Adam tried not to stare at the shapely line of her figure.

He didn't understand his reaction to this woman. He normally loved blond, petite, delicate women. But Maureen York was none of those things. She was tall, with a full, ripe figure. She was downright curvy. Her hair and eyes were both dark. And, God help him, she was the sexiest woman he'd ever encountered.

"Look, Maureen—either you want to stay in a boring motel room, or you want to come out to the ranch. Which will it be?"

She glanced at him. "I don't want to be a problem for any of you."

Adam shrugged. "One more mouth to feed won't put us out."

"You really know how to make a woman feel...wanted."

A smug smile dimpled one of his cheeks. "I've been told that before."

Dear Reader,

As spring turns to summer, make Silhouette Romance the perfect companion for those lazy days and sultry nights! Fans of our LOVING THE BOSS series won't want to miss *The Marriage Merger* by exciting author Vivian Leiber. A pretend engagement between friends goes awry when their white lies lead to a *real* white wedding!

Take one biological-clock-ticking twin posing as a new mom and one daddy determined to gain custody of his newborn son, and you've got the unsuspecting partners in *The Baby Arrangement,* Moyra Tarling's tender BUNDLES OF JOY title. You've asked for more TWINS ON THE DOORSTEP, Stella Bagwell's charming author-led miniseries, so this month we give you *Millionaire on Her Doorstep,* an emotional story of two wounded souls who find love in the most unexpected way...and in the most unexpected place.

Can a bachelor bent on never marrying and a single mom with a bustling brood of four become a *Fairy-Tale Family?* Find out in Pat Montana's delightful new novel. Next, a handsome doctor's case of mistaken identity leads to *The Triplet's Wedding Wish* in this heartwarming tale by DeAnna Talcott. And a young widow finds the home—and family—she's always wanted when she strikes a deal with a *Nevada Cowboy Dad,* this month's FAMILY MATTERS offering from Dorsey Kelley.

Enjoy this month's fantastic selections, and make sure to return each and every month to Silhouette Romance!

Mary-Theresa Hussey

Mary-Theresa Hussey
Senior Editor, Silhouette Romance

Please address questions and book requests to:
Silhouette Reader Service
U.S.: 3010 Walden Ave., P.O. Box 1325, Buffalo, NY 14269
Canadian: P.O. Box 609, Fort Erie, Ont. L2A 5X3

Stella Bagwell

MILLIONAIRE ON HER DOORSTEP

Silhouette
ROMANCE™
Published by Silhouette Books
America's Publisher of Contemporary Romance

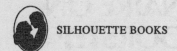

SILHOUETTE BOOKS

ISBN 0-373-19368-8

MILLIONAIRE ON HER DOORSTEP

Books by Stella Bagwell

STELLA BAGWELL

sold her first book to Silhouette in November 1985. Now, more than thirty novels later, she is still thrilled to see her books in print and can't imagine having any other job than that of writing about two people falling in love.

She lives in a small town in southeastern Oklahoma with her husband of twenty-six years. She has one son.

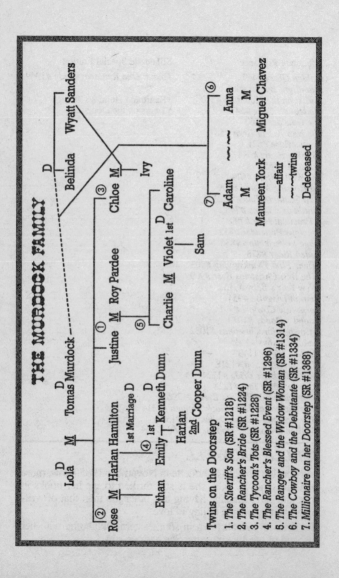

THE MURDOCK FAMILY

Lola —M— Tomas Murdock (D) ------ Belinda —D— Wyatt Sanders

Rose —M— Harlan Hamilton (1st Marriage D)

Justine —M— Roy Pardee ①

Chloe —M— Ivy ③

② Ethan —M—

Harlan Hamilton (1st) Kenneth Dunn (D) ④ 1st

Emily —T— Kenneth Dunn (D)

Harlan 1st
Cooper Dunn 2nd

Charlie —M— Violet (1st) —D— Caroline ⑤

Sam

Adam —M— Maureen York ⑦

Anna —M— Miguel Chavez ⑥

——— affair
~~~ twins
D—deceased

Twins on the Doorstep

Chapter One

"You're not going to use that thing on me!" Horrified, Adam stared at his aunt Justine as though he was certain the woman had lost her mind. The tall redhead had worked as an R.N. in Ruidoso's medical clinic for years and was famed for her gentle, expert care with patients. But at the moment, Adam thought she looked more like a perfect assistant for Dr. Frankenstein.

The older woman pulled the trigger on the electric machine in her hand and the jigsaw blade buzzed loudly. "I know it looks like something I pulled off a carpenter's truck, but believe me, if you want that cast off your leg sometime before lunch, you'll have to trust me. Otherwise, I'll have to get out the old handsaw."

His eyes riveted on the buzzing blade, he asked, "You can't put something on the plaster to melt it off? Water? Bourbon? Acid?"

She chuckled. "You big, strong men are all alike.

Scared to death of a little needle. Keel over in a dead faint at the first sign of blood. If it was left up to you males to have the babies, the world population would quickly dwindle.''

Justine grabbed his foot and propped the blob of white plaster against her thigh. Adam clutched the edges of the examining table and braced himself for what was to come.

"If it was left up to me…" He stopped, his breath lodged in his throat as Justine guided the blade into the cast. White dust boiled as the saw ate through the chalky material.

"If what was left up to you?" his aunt prompted as she guided the blade up and over the region of his ankle.

Trying not to think of his newly healed bone being cut in half, Adam said, "The world population *would* be zero. I don't ever intend to have kids."

Justine made a clucking noise of disapproval. "Your mother would kick you in the rear if she could hear you."

"She probably would," Adam agreed. "But I've told her Anna and Ivy can give her grandchildren. No need to count on me to keep the Murdock and Sanders bloodlines going."

With the cast cut from one end to the other, Justine set the electric saw aside and carefully pried the plaster away from his foot. Adam was relieved to finally see his ankle and foot were still intact after six long weeks of imprisonment.

She rubbed her hand over his ankle and the top of his foot, then seemingly satisfied he was healed, she smiled up at him. "You have a thing against babies and children?" Justine asked him.

"Actually, I like kids. But having them without a wife doesn't work well. And I don't want one of those. I don't want a woman telling me when to get up, when to eat, when to go to bed, how to spend my time or money."

With her hands on her hips, his aunt stepped back and pinned him with an admonishing look. "You've never had a wife. What makes you think we do all those things?"

He let out a tiresome groan. Justine and his mother, Chloe, were sisters. In all likelihood, this conversation would be discussed between the two of them. He really should make an effort to choose his words more wisely. But why bother? His mother already knew his feelings on the matter.

"Oh, I hear things from my married buddies. And I've had a few girlfriends who gave me plenty of clues as to what it would be like to have a woman permanently attached to me," he told her. Then with a grimace, he swiped a hand through his dark auburn hair. The loose wave flopped once again on his forehead. "That's not to say I think marriage is a bad thing. After all, Charlie seems to love being a husband and father. And now my sister, Anna, is walking around in a fog of wedded bliss. But I'm convinced none of that is for me."

Justine tapped a forefinger against her chin as she carefully studied her nephew. "I've never been one to meddle in your life, Adam."

"So don't spoil your record by doing it now," he retorted.

Ignoring his tone of warning, Justine said, "The past few years you've gone through women as if they were a stack of shirts to be tried on for size."

Adam snorted. "That's right. And none of them fitted."

Justine sighed. "I know you don't believe it, Adam, but there is a special woman out there for you."

"No, Aunt Justine, that's where you're wrong. All the special ones are taken. One way or the other."

They both knew he was talking about Susan's death. But thankfully she decided now wasn't the time to bring up Adam's tragic loss.

Justine patted his shoulder. "Don't get too cross with me. It's just that your old aunt is more concerned about your mental health than the state of that skinny foot of yours."

Adam glanced wryly at his bare foot. "My mental health is dandy now that I'm back in New Mexico. And don't go comparing my foot with Charlie's. That son of yours should've been a football player instead of a Texas Ranger. The profession would've been a helluva lot safer, if you ask me."

Justine smiled impishly. "A helluva lot," she agreed, then pointed to his newly mended bones. "But it appears to me that being an oilman isn't all that safe, either. I can't ever remember Charlie going around on crutches for six weeks."

Leaning forward, Adam gave the vinyl padding on the examining table a loud slap. "You just made a good point, Aunt Justine. Being an oilman didn't cause my ankle to get broken. A woman did this to me!"

One of Justine's brows arched with wry amusement. "Really? I thought you got hurt on the job."

Adam shot her a tired look. "It *was* on the job! The woman was crazy...." He broke off with a shake of his head, and Justine laughed. "Oh, go get the doctor, would you? I'm supposed to meet Dad in twenty minutes."

Laughing softly, she turned to leave the examining room. "Okay, I'll let you off the hook this time. But one of these days I want to hear how you actually broke that ankle."

When Adam arrived at the offices of Sanders Gas and Exploration thirty minutes later, he bypassed the receptionist and three secretaries, went straight to his father's office and rapped his knuckles against the dark oak door.

Behind the wooden panel he could hear muffled voices. Good, he thought. The new geologist his father had hired was already here and hopefully ready to go to work. There were a lot of new projects waiting for decisions to be made, and now that he was free of the cumbersome cast on his foot, he was raring to get started on them.

A second later, the door opened. His father, Wyatt, still handsome and dark-headed at the age of fifty-five, grabbed him by the shoulder and pulled him into the large office.

"Adam! Come in. I was wondering if you were going to make it," he exclaimed with cheerful affection. "I see you finally got that damn cast off. How does your ankle feel?"

Adam glanced to his left where a desk and several pieces of leather furniture were grouped near a glass wall. The toe of a heavy work boot and part of a leg encased in faded denim peeked out from one of the chairs, but the high back prevented a clear view of the person sitting in front of Wyatt's desk.

Turning his attention back to his father, Adam said, "Right now, my ankle is as stiff and swollen as the fat end of a baseball bat. I had to cut the instep of my boot with a pocketknife just to get the damn thing on. A five-hundred-dollar pair of ostrich boots at that! But the doctor says it's healed and it'll soon get back to normal. I just hope the man knows what he's talking about."

The older man gave Adam's shoulder an encouraging slap. "You'll be able to run a footrace in a couple of weeks. And as for the ostrich boots, they're not nearly as valuable as your neck."

Adam chuckled grimly as Wyatt nudged his son toward the desk and accompanying chairs. "Come on. I want you to meet our new geologist. I believe you two are going to work wonders together."

The chair slowly swiveled to face the two men, and Adam instantly halted in his tracks.

"You!"

He very nearly shouted the one word as the woman rose gracefully to her feet. She was exactly as he remembered. Tall, long-legged, with curves that were full and lusty. Her long brown hair was thick and coarse and streaked by too much time in the sun. At the moment, it was braided in the same way his mother braided the tails of her horses before a muddy race.

"You two know each other?" Wyatt asked. With a puzzled frown, he glanced from his son to the woman he'd just invited into the company.

"This is your son?" she asked Wyatt in a voice as husky as Adam remembered.

His eyes traveled from the rope of hair lying against the jut of one breast to the look of disbelief on her face. "As if you didn't already know!" Adam drawled mockingly.

Ignoring him, she turned dark brown eyes on Wyatt. "I thought your name was Sanders."

"It is," the older man assured her.

She looked at Adam, and he suddenly felt as if a boot heel had landed in the middle of his gut.

"Down in South America, you were introduced to me as Adam Murdock," she said, her voice full of confusion.

"I am Adam Murdock," he snarled. "Adam Murdock Sanders. Don't try to tell me you didn't know."

"Adam!" Wyatt exclaimed. "What's the matter with you? Ms. York hasn't done anything to you!"

"The hell she hasn't! She very nearly killed me. She put me in the hospital and my foot in a cast for more than six weeks!"

Sparks flew from Maureen York's dark eyes as she pinned him with a glare that would have withered a lesser man. "I didn't do anything to you! You did it to yourself!"

"Sure. I'm the one who swerved to miss that damn dog!"

Her brows shot up with indignation. "Would you have had me kill it?"

"That would've been a helluva lot better than killing me!"

A deep shade of rose spread across her high cheekbones. "Nothing would've happened to you if you'd been wearing your seat belt. Like I told you to in the first place. But no. You had to play macho man and—"

"I wouldn't have—"

"Whoa! Whoa now!" Wyatt shouted above their voices. "I think there's been a mistake here and—"

"There sure has," Adam interrupted hotly. "And the mistake was hiring this—" he gestured toward Maureen "—this maniac."

"I'm sorry, Mr. Sanders," Maureen spoke up. "I didn't realize this—" she inclined her head toward Adam "—this man was your son. Otherwise, I would've saved the time and trouble for both of us and told you I couldn't accept the position in your company."

Seeing the whole situation was escalating out of control, Wyatt shook his head at her. "Please take a seat, Maureen, while I have a word with Adam. It won't be but a few minutes. I promise."

She weighed his plea for a moment, then with a reluctant nod returned to the chair she'd been sitting in earlier. As for Adam, Wyatt hustled him out the door and down the hallway to a storeroom.

"What in hell's come over you?" Wyatt shot at him the moment the door closed behind the two men. "I've never seen you act so rude and overbearing in my life! Ms. York is a damned good geologist. One of the very best. We're lucky to be getting her. If we still are. Thanks to you."

Adam deeply respected his father and loved him even more. From the time he was a small boy, he'd known he wanted to grow up and be just like him. He'd wanted to be an oilman and a damned good one. He wanted to be known the way Wyatt was in the business. But there were times he clashed with the older man, and this just happened to be one of them.

"Dad, Maureen York is the woman who was driving me out to the rig site down in South America.

She was the woman who wrecked me. Do I need to say more?''

Wyatt rolled his eyes. "Adam, you know the woman didn't purposely wreck the Jeep to hurt you. And I had no idea the Maureen woman you'd mentioned that day in the hospital was this one! You only told me she was giving you a lift out to the rig. I didn't know she was a geologist or even that she worked for an oil company. I thought it was some girlfriend you'd picked up down there and she was simply giving you a ride!''

"She was giving me a ride all right!" he growled, then seeing the impatient look on his father's face, he let out a heavy sigh. "Look, Dad, even if she didn't intentionally wreck the Jeep, she has a list of other problems. Frankly, I don't think I could work with her for two days, or even two hours.''

Wyatt folded his arms across his chest and leveled a stern look on his son's face. "All right, tell me what sort of problems she has.''

"She's reckless. Opinionated. Stubborn. And disrespectful.''

"In other words, she's a whole lot like you.''

Adam shook his head. "Dad, you know what I mean. She's—well, she's a woman in a man's world. She doesn't fit.''

"She's smarter than any man I've come across. She'll be a big asset to the company.''

"Find me someone else to work with and you can cut my salary in half.''

Wyatt's brows shot up. "You're serious!''

"Damn serious," Adam told him.

Wyatt studied him for long moments. He'd seen that look on his son's face before. Stubborn, defiant, even a little reckless. And he felt as if thirty years had rolled back and he was staring at himself in the mirror.

"Well, I'm serious, too," Wyatt told him. "I can see you're letting your personal feelings get in the way of the real purpose here. To get gas and oil from the ground and eventually to the consumer."

Ducking his head, Adam jammed his hands in the front pockets of his jeans and stared at the toes of his cowboy boots. His *ruined* cowboy boots. But he tried not to think about that now. He could probably forget that Maureen had slung him out of that open-topped Jeep, too. But could he bear to be around her day in, day out? The woman bothered him in ways he didn't want to think about.

"I have no personal feelings for Maureen York," he said bluntly.

"It didn't sound like that a few moments ago when you were practically biting her head off," Wyatt pointed out. "Did the two of you...you didn't come on to the woman down there in South America, did you?"

Adam appeared shocked by his father's question. "Dad, Ms. York is probably getting close to thirty!"

Wyatt's expression grew wry. "Since when did a few years' difference in ages ever stop you?"

Adam had the grace to blush. "Well, maybe she isn't that much older than me. But I can safely say she's...far from my type."

"Good." Wyatt gave Adam's shoulder an encouraging pat. "Then it won't be a problem for you to go back into my office and assure her you're looking forward to working with her."

"I'll do my best to lie like hell."

Wyatt chuckled. "Trust me, Adam, in a few months' time, you'll be thanking me for hiring the woman."

Maureen had almost decided not to wait another minute when the door to the office swung open and Adam Murdock Sanders entered the room. She immediately rose to her feet and clasped her hands behind her back.

"Where is Mr. Sanders?" she asked him without preamble.

"I'm the Mr. Sanders you'll be working with. My father has gone home to our ranch."

Maureen moistened her lips and told herself to remain calm. She'd never been an emotional woman. It was one of the reasons she was successful in spite of her gender. But there was something about this young man that got under her skin like no one ever had.

"Look, Mr. San—Mr. Murdock Sanders," she corrected pointedly, "I believe you and I both know we could never work together."

Adam totally agreed. But as his father had voiced a few minutes ago, this was one time he was going to have to put his personal feelings aside. This earthy-looking woman was a highly intelligent scientist. He'd been around her for less than a day, but the short time had been enough for him to conclude she'd known her business.

He walked to the desk and propped one hip on the corner. "I'm willing to try."

"Because your father is forcing you to?"

Adam tried not to bristle at her question. "Wyatt doesn't force me to do anything. He isn't that sort of father. And I'm not that sort of son."

Looking at him, Maureen could well believe he

wasn't a man to be pushed around. In spite of his young years, he already had more presence than a man had a right to possess. And it wasn't just his physical appearance. Though heaven knew how the sight of his lean, broad-shouldered body shook her right to the marrow of her bones.

"Yes, I can believe that. I can't see you bending to anyone."

Adam's gaze searched her face for a clue as to where her thinking was headed. Yet somewhere along the way he forgot why he was looking. Instead, he began to take account of her high cheekbones, smooth golden skin and chocolate-brown eyes. Her wide, full lips were stained with cherry-red lipstick, and the bright contrast against the rest of her bare face was the most erotic thing Adam could remember seeing on a woman.

Deliberately clearing his throat, he said, "Look, Ms. York, I realize we don't know each other that well and—"

"Four hours at the most," she interrupted.

Adam nodded, then feeling as if the office was closing in on him, he turned and walked over to a small table holding a coffee machine, paper cups and other fixings.

"Would you like coffee? Or there's a soda machine at the front of the building," he offered.

"Coffee will be fine," she accepted. "Leave it black."

He poured two cups and carried one to her. He'd intended to simply hand it over, then move away. But as he'd discovered in the short time he'd been with her in South America, his intentions went awry whenever he was near Maureen York. Instead, he remained less than a step away from her, his eyes going once again to her red lips. "I...understand you really weren't trying to kill me. It just seemed that way."

"Believe me, Mr. Sanders, if I'd been trying to murder you, I'd have found an easier, more thorough way than slinging you out of an open-topped Jeep." She sipped the coffee, grimaced at the bitter taste, then leveled her eyes on his face. He had strong, bony features, darkly tanned skin and eyes as green as a wet emerald. His hair was the rich color of polished mahogany and flopped onto his forehead in a thick wave. If she had to describe his looks in one word, it would have to be sexy.

"Do you actually believe we can work together?" she asked him.

Adam couldn't imagine getting any sort of work done while in this woman's company. But he was going to keep that opinion to himself. Sanders Exploration needed a good geologist in a bad way. If it had to be Maureen York, then he'd do his best to be a professional about it.

"I can forget our first meeting if you can," he said.

She smelled like lilacs on a warm summer night, and before Adam could stop them, all sorts of questions about her were running through his mind.

"How generous of you," she replied.

A pent-up breath drained out of him. If his memory served him right, she'd told him she was divorced and that she'd worked as a geologist for nearly ten years. Other than that, he knew nothing about where she'd come from or how his father had managed to ferret her out of a long list of potential candidates for the job.

"I'm trying to be," he agreed.

Maureen took another sip of coffee. "I, uh, the next day after the accident, I was on my way to the hospital to check on you, but an unexpected call forced me to turn around and head to the airport to catch a plane back to the States. I called the hospital later, and a nurse assured me you were going to be fine. I was glad."

Back in the hospital, Adam had told himself he didn't care if Maureen York had the courtesy to see if he was going to live or die. But now...well, hell, he felt like he was fifteen instead of twenty-five. It was downright ridiculous how much better her explanation made him feel.

"I have been...fine. Just hampered with a cast." He forced himself to move away from her.

At the corner of the desk, he picked up his coffee cup and carried it over to the glass wall. The pine- and spruce-covered mountains spread in a panoramic view to the south. Reluctantly, he kept his eyes on their beauty rather than Maureen York's.

"What brought you here to Sanders Exploration?" he asked. "Six weeks ago, you obviously had a job with a good company."

Maureen was wondering the same thing herself. She hadn't been unhappy with her former employers. Their headquarters were based in Houston and you couldn't get any closer to the oil and gas industry than that. She'd been paid a top-notch salary and the people she worked with had been easy to deal with. But she'd been feeling stifled by the city. And though she hated to admit it, she'd had to face the fact that her life had grown stagnant. She wanted and needed a change. Still—if she'd had any idea this man was a part of Sanders Exploration, she never would have agreed to hire on.

"For one thing, I wanted to get out of Houston. I didn't dislike the city, but I was tired of living in an apartment and dealing with the fast pace. I want a house with a yard and trees."

He couldn't stop his eyes from cutting over his shoulder at her. "Sounds like you want to settle down rather than gear up for work."

Squaring her shoulders, she walked around the desk and joined him at the windows. "I guess you could say I'd like to slow down. But not in the way you're thinking."

His dark green eyes met her brown ones. "I didn't know there was any other way for a...woman."

Her nostrils flared as she wondered why anything this man could say or think should matter to her. True, she would have to work with him, but she'd dealt with far worse. So why did she let his little innuendos fire her temper? It was silly.

"You might be interested to know that all of us women aren't pining to get married. We can have a life without a man."

"Really? My mother thinks a woman has to be with a man and a man has to be with a woman before they can ever be truly happy."

Something about his voice, the way he talked about men and women made her feel as if she were a very young teenage girl just learning how it felt to be flirted with by a handsome boy. Yet Adam Sanders was far from being a boy, and she had long since passed the flirting teenage years.

"Your mother must be a hopeless romantic," she murmured, then turned away from him and settled her gaze on the mountains stretching for several miles in the distance.

And Maureen York wasn't a romantic. She hadn't said the words, but Adam had read them on her face just before she'd turned her head away. Well, that was fine, even good, he thought. It was a relief to know she wasn't searching for romance. It would make their job together so much easier.

"This job will send you to all sorts of places, particularly here in New Mexico. It's not likely you're going to get much time to spend in that house with a yard."

She looked at him from the corner of her eye. "You don't want me to take this job, do you?"

Fearing she could read his expression, Adam kept his gaze firmly entrenched on the view outside the glass wall. When his father had purchased this office building more than twenty years ago, he'd also bought several adjoining lots to keep any sort of neighbors at bay. To this day, beautiful woods of pine, spruce and aspen grew right up to the back of the building, and at most any time of the day, chipmunks and birds could be seen feeding right outside the windows.

"I don't have the final say-so whether you work here or not. My father has that right," he told her.

"That's not what I said," she pointed out.

"I think you've come here searching for something you couldn't find in Houston. I don't think you'll find it here, either."

How could he know what she was searching for? Maureen wondered crossly. She swallowed the last of the bitter coffee and tossed the cup in a trash can sitting next to the desk. "Are you an authority on geologists or women or both?"

"I don't profess to be an authority on anything," he retorted.

She smiled, but the expression didn't reach her eyes. "Then don't try to figure me out. More than one man has tried it and failed."

That got his instant attention, and he twisted around and pinned her with a stare of disbelief. "Look, Ms. York, I'm not trying to analyze you. I just want to make sure you're here to work. This may not be like the huge company you worked for in Houston, but we do sink a lot of holes. If you came out here thinking this job was going to be easy, then you might as well head back to Texas."

She walked to within a step of him, folded her arms across her breasts and looked up at him. "How old are you, Mr. Sanders?"

He frowned as though he couldn't believe her question. "Twenty-five. Not that my age has anything to do with this conversation!"

"Hmm. Well, I was just amazed that you got so smart in such a short length of time. It takes most men many more years than you've acquired."

Adam could rightly say without a drop of conceit that he'd always found it easy to converse with women, to charm and cajole them around to his way of thinking. He normally had a gift for gab. Especially with the opposite sex. A trait he'd been told he inherited from his birth father, Tomas Murdock, who'd died shortly after he was born. But this woman was not like any he'd encountered before. He wanted to kiss her and strangle her. He wanted to shake the haughty confidence from her face.

She dropped her arms, and his eyes fell to the generous line of her breasts. Beneath the mint-green cotton shirt, he could see the faint outline of her lacy bra. He tried not to think how she would look without either piece of clothing.

"I guess you could say I'm a…fast learner," he drawled.

Noticing the line of his vision had strayed lower than her face, Maureen folded her arms back over her breasts and glared at him. "I can tell you right now, the only reason I'm going to stay with Sanders Exploration is your father. He's a man who's highly admired in this business, and now that I've met him, I can see why. I'm flattered to have the chance to work for him. And I've decided it would be foolish to throw it away just because he has a cocky, know-it-all son."

His brows lifted as his lips spread into a devilish grin. "So this means we'll be working together?"

"Against my better judgment."

It was certainly against Adam's judgment, too. But he wasn't a man to back away from a challenge. "My dad will be pleased to hear it."

She smiled then. A sumptuous little movement of her lips that packed enough power to curl Adam's toes.

"You don't have to bother saying you're pleased, too," she countered.

As if she considered their conversation closed, she walked over to the chair she'd been sitting in and picked up a leather purse. She pulled the strap onto her shoulder and started to the door. Adam's gaze followed the graceful swing of her hips.

"Do you need help finding a place around here?" he asked in afterthought.

She glanced at her wristwatch, then opened the door. "I'm meeting a real-estate agent in thirty minutes."

"A real-estate agent! You mean you're planning to buy rather than rent?"

She smiled again. "You said Sanders Exploration sinks a lot of holes—well, I plan to sink some roots."

"Without a trial run?"

She nodded. "The moment I saw this area, I fell in love with it. In the past few minutes, I've decided that whatever I have to put up with on the job will be a small price to pay to make my home here."

My home. She'd told Adam she wasn't seeking a home in the traditional sense. So what *was* she looking for? And why did he keep picturing her as a wife and mother? She was a scientist. A woman who studied rocks and shale and sludge and seismographic charts.

"Then I hope you're not disappointed, Ms. York."

"The only way I'll be disappointed is if you continue to call me Ms. York. My name is Maureen," she said with a wry smile, then slipped past the door and out of Adam's sight.

Adam thrust a hand through his hair and let out a low groan. The woman was a walking piece of dynamite. Just looking at her was dangerous. And working with her? Well, he could already see the explosion coming.

Chapter Two

The sky was full of stars and a warm breeze carried the scent of sage and pine. The sweeter fragrance of petunias blooming close by mingled with the tangy smells of the high desert country.

It was a pleasant night to eat outdoors, and for the first time in ages, his parents had managed to find time in their busy schedules to meet him at this favorite mountainside restaurant.

Across the table, Chloe was finishing the last of her chocolate mousse while the two men sipped their coffee. "I know you're ready to go, darling," she said to Wyatt. "But just give me time for a few more bites. It's rare I have a chance to eat a dessert I haven't made myself."

Wyatt chuckled and patted his wife's hand. "I know, you're just a regular little slave. One of these days, I might let you out of your chains."

A faint smile crossed Adam's face as he watched the teasing exchange between his parents. After twenty-some years of marriage, the two of them were still very much in love and completely devoted to each other. The solidity of his family had always been reassuring to Adam. Yet now that he'd grown older, his parents' relationship oftentimes amazed him. And sometimes even saddened him. Because he knew he would never be blessed in such a way.

Chloe put down her spoon and dabbed her lips with her napkin. "Okay, signal the waiter for the check and we'll get out of here," she told her husband. "I need to get home anyway and check on that mare. If she doesn't foal tonight, she will tomorrow."

Wyatt reached for his wallet and began to thumb through the bills inside. Across the table, Adam shook his head. "Forget the check," he told the two of them. "I'm footing the bill."

His mother frowned at him. "Adam, this is a celebration of sorts because you got your cast off. Your dad and I want to treat you."

"Having your company was treat enough."

Wyatt put his wallet away, then scraped back his chair and patted his nonexistent belly. "Well, I must admit this has been a good day. My son got his foot back, the company just hired the best damn geologist in the gas business, and now I've had a free meal to top it all off."

"Well, if Miss Mighty Dash gives me the painted colt I want, then it will be a perfect day," Chloe added as she fished her purse from beneath the chair.

"By the way," Wyatt said to Adam, "do you know if Ms. York has a place to stay yet?"

"She mentioned something about meeting with a real-estate agent this afternoon," Adam told him. "I suppose for right now, she's staying in a motel."

Wyatt gave his chin a thoughtful rub. "She's taking on a major relocation to work for us. We really should invite her to stay on the ranch until she can find a more permanent place and get her things shipped up from Houston. What do you think?" He turned a questioning look on his wife.

Chloe smiled agreeably. "We've had some of your other employees stay at the ranch before. As far as I'm concerned, Ms. York is certainly welcome."

Adam stared at the two of them in utter dismay. Normally, it wouldn't make any difference to him who stayed on the Bar M. The ranch was his parents' home. Adam had his own place. But this past month he'd temporarily moved back to the Bar M while a pair of carpenters renovated the inside of his house. If Maureen moved out to the Bar M, that meant he'd have to live with her, too!

"You can't be serious! She doesn't need to be invited to the Bar M! No way! No how! Look, I may have to work with her, but that doesn't mean I have to be in her company round the clock!"

"Why, Adam," Chloe scolded, taken aback by her son's sudden outburst, "Ms. York wouldn't necessarily be your guest. She'd be your dad's and mine. What's with all the uproar anyway? It's not like you to be so petty and childish."

There wasn't anything childish about the feelings Maureen York stirred up in him, and he was relieved that the shadows of the evening were settling over the restaurant's outdoor patio; otherwise, his parents would see a blush pouring over his face.

"Mother, I'm not being childish. The woman...well, we just rub each other the wrong way.

Believe me, you don't want that much friction in the house."

She studied him thoughtfully, and just when Adam was certain she was going to accuse him of behaving boorishly, she surprised him by saying, "All right, Adam, I'm sure your dad will agree that we don't want to force the woman down your throat. If that's the way you feel, we'll let her stay in a motel and the company can reimburse her for her expenses."

"It's the way I feel," he clipped.

Chloe and Wyatt rose to their feet, thanked him for the meal and bade him good-night. By the time they started to walk away from the table, Adam felt as if he'd shrunk to the height of two inches.

"Wait a minute," he called out to them.

Both his parents paused and glanced back at him. "Was there something else you wanted to say about Ms. York?" Wyatt asked with an innocence that irked Adam.

"Hell, yes! I'll invite her out to the ranch myself! But don't be surprised if she refuses to come. I think the woman would take particular pleasure in killing me."

Chloe smiled sweetly at her son. "Well, darling, I'm sure she's not the first woman who's wanted to kill you."

Maureen hated motel rooms. In the past nine or ten years, she'd spent many nights in the dreaded places. Some had been luxurious, others cheap. But no matter the price or how many of her personal things she had lying about, it was still a sterile room. Just a place to sleep, shower and dress.

She snorted inwardly. Since when had her apartment in Houston ever been more than just a place to hang her clothes and lay her head? And what made her think things would be any different here in New Mexico?

From the middle of the queen-size bed, Maureen aimed the remote at the television and smashed the Off button. For the past hour and a half, she'd been staring at the flickering screen, yet she didn't have a clue as to what she'd been watching. Her mind had been on the place she'd left, this place she'd come to. And the man she was going to have to face in the morning.

Adam Murdock Sanders. Who'd have ever thought she'd run into him again? That morning down in South America, she'd met him quite by chance. He'd been having coffee in the hotel restaurant with a tool pusher who worked for the same company as Maureen. He'd introduced her to Adam, and while the three of them had coffee, she'd learned his rented vehicle had quit and he needed to be at a rig site before noon.

The town they'd been staying in was too small for a car rental agency or a mechanic who wasn't already busy. Knowing all this, the tool pusher had urged Maureen into being a Good Samaritan and offering Adam a lift. Everything afterward had gone from bad to worse.

Adam had refused to wear his seat belt, complained about her fast, reckless driving, then went on to imply she'd be doing the world a much bigger favor if she would stay home to raise her "kids" rather than traipse around with a bunch of foul-mouthed oilmen.

Well, he'd had the mouth for the business, all right. And she'd wanted to knock his head off his shoulders.

But she'd truly never meant to hurt him. The dog had run into the narrow, graveled road without any warning, and Maureen had instinctively jerked the wheel to miss it. Adam had gone flying out the open door, landing on the shoulder of the road before rolling to the bottom of a steep bar ditch.

At first, she'd been terrified she'd killed him. But to her amazement he'd managed, with her help, to make it up the embankment and into the Jeep. Maureen had driven him to the nearest hospital more than fifty miles away, then waited until a nurse had come to assure her he was fine and the doctor had already plastered his broken ankle.

Maureen had asked to see him, but the nurse informed her he'd been sedated and was expected to sleep for several hours. She'd had no choice but to leave. The next day she'd been driving back to the hospital to see him when her boss from Houston had called and ordered her home immediately.

Back in Texas, she'd reported the accident to her company so Adam's medical bills would be rightly taken care of by insurance, then she'd tried to put the whole incident out of her mind. But forgetting the young company man hadn't been that easy. She'd thought about him most every day since. Maybe that was one of the reasons she'd been so shocked this morning when he'd walked into Wyatt Sanders's office.

With a troubled sigh, she left the bed, grabbed her keys from the built-in dresser and walked out the door. With no thought to the lateness of the hour, she climbed into her pickup truck and headed toward the main highway. For several minutes, she traveled west, up into the mountains, before eventually pulling onto a graveled road.

The real-estate sign at the edge of the highway was already marked Sold. Maureen had only given the agent a verbal "I'll take it," but the flimsy commitment was enough to make her wonder if she was being a mite hasty. Or, even worse, going crazy.

A mite hasty! Whom was she kidding? A normal person didn't go out and buy the first house they looked at! And as for her going crazy, she had to be cracking up to think she could ever have a real home here in southern New Mexico or anywhere. When her husband had walked out on her, she'd seen the last of her hopes and dreams vanish. Since then, she'd finally come to the conclusion that it was foolish of her to ever plan on having a real home with a family.

The long, graveled lane curved, then made one last switch back before the house came into view. The split-level structure had been built on a rough ledge of the mountain. There was hardly a yard to speak of. Unless you counted the rocks and clumps of sage clinging tenaciously to the ground sloping down to the driveway.

Tall pine and aspen dappled the pink stucco walls and red tiled roof with gently moving shadows. The prickly beauty of blooming cholla cactus guarded the front entrance.

Maureen parked the pickup on the graveled circle driveway and slipped quietly to the ground. The mountain air had already grown incredibly cool for midsummer and she wrapped her arms around herself to ward off the chill as she climbed a set of simple rock stepping stones up the sloping yard.

This wasn't Houston by any means. From now on

she would have to remember she was seven thousand feet or more above sea level and needed to keep a jacket with her after dark. And compared to the busy, humid city, the quietness here on the mountaintop was nearly deafening. Other than the wind whispering through the pine boughs and rattling the aspen leaves, there were no other sounds.

She smiled to herself as she imagined what her friends back in Houston would think about her buying such a secluded home. Probably that she was asking for trouble. And she doubted any of her female friends would have driven up here alone at this late hour. But Maureen wasn't afraid.

For nearly ten years she'd been on her own. Alone. Facing the world without her husband or her child. She couldn't possibly be hurt any worse than when they'd gone out of her life.

Maureen wandered around the house, studying its strong walls and gracefully arched windows trimmed with dark wood. It was a lovely structure, but the house or even the wild, beautiful tangle of forest growing around it was not the thing that had called to her when she'd first seen the place. Job or not. Family or not. She'd simply felt a deep intuition that here in New Mexico was where she belonged. And in spite of Adam Sanders, this was where she was going to stay.

The next morning, Maureen was already at work when Adam arrived at Sanders Gas and Exploration. He found her in the small lab behind his office. She was standing at a cabinet counter, the sleeves of her blue striped shirt rolled above her elbows, a pair of gold-framed glasses on her nose. Once again her brown hair was braided. The single rope reached the waistband at the back of her jeans. He wondered how long her hair would be if she let it loose, or if she ever did.

Hearing his step, Maureen glanced up from the seismographic chart she'd been studying and peered at him from behind the lenses of her glasses.

"Good morning," she said warmly.

Encouraged by her greeting, he joined her at the counter. Just because the woman stirred his libido didn't mean he lacked manners or enough sense to accomplish a day's work, he assured himself. If she could be civil and productive, he certainly could.

"Good morning," he replied, then inclined his head toward the charts on the counter. "I see you've already found something to work on."

"These are the first tests from several sections of land in eastern Oklahoma." She tapped a set of papers with her forefinger, then reached for another stack lying nearby. "These are from an area in northern New Mexico. Both I'd wager to produce gas. I just don't know how much yet."

One corner of his mouth curved wryly. "Wager? You're not here to make bets, Ms. York. You're here to show us scientific evidence."

Maureen glanced at the small watch on her wrist. "I've been at work forty-five minutes. How quickly am I supposed to produce this scientific evidence? Within an hour? Or are you going to be considerate and give me until the end of the day?"

He grinned slyly. "I'm not a patient man. I like things done yesterday. But since this is your first day here at Sanders, I'll make allowances."

A closer look at his face told Maureen he was teasing, and that surprised her about the man. The only way she'd ever seen him was serious and driven. She'd expected his biting attitude of yesterday to be his usual disposition and she wasn't sure this warmer, more congenial Adam was any easier to take than the infuriating man she'd confronted in Wyatt's office.

Pulling her glasses from her face, she placed them gently atop the charts. "Your father tells me several more seismograph holes are going to be shot this week on the Oklahoma land. He wants me to read those before we fly back there for a look."

"We" more than likely meant Adam and Maureen. He didn't know how he was going to manage traveling with her. But he had to. It was a big part of their job going from one potential well site to the next. Hopefully, the strong reactions he had to her now would quickly fade. Maybe tomorrow or the next day, he'd be able to look at her and not wonder what it would be like to have her in his arms.

"It'll be rough, mountainous terrain. Have you been there before?"

With a shake of her head, she moved away from him. "I've been mostly doing overseas or offshore work."

Adam watched her walk over to a long table and pick up a paper cup filled with coffee. From a paper sack on the counter, she pulled out a raspberry Danish.

"There's a doughnut left in the sack if you want it," she offered as she took a seat on a folding metal chair.

"Thanks, but I've already had breakfast."

No doubt, Maureen thought. He'd probably had a regular meal sitting in a kitchen or dining room. "I suppose you wouldn't stoop to putting something like this in your system,'' she said.

A faint smile tilting his lips, he shook his head. ''Not near enough grease to suit me. Give me *chorizo* or bacon and eggs.''

''Surely you know that isn't good for you,'' she said, her gaze following him as he went over to the small coffeepot sitting on the cabinet counter. He was dressed not as a businessman who worked in oil, but as a rancher, in black boots and faded blue jeans that hugged his hips and thighs. A denim shirt of deep green covered his muscular torso. The rugged clothing emphasized his fitness and mocked the fact he didn't eat health food. It also mocked Maureen's vow never to look at another man in a purely physical way.

''My mom tells me that very thing every morning,'' Adam said, ''but she cooks the stuff for me anyway.''

The cup in her hand stopped midway to her lips. ''You still live at home?''

He grimaced as he poured himself a cup of the strong brew. ''You make it sound like a crime.''

She didn't know where the defensive tone in his voice was coming from. She hadn't accused him of being a pup still latched onto his mother's teat.

''Not at all.'' She studied him carefully as he took a seat across from her. ''I just thought...well, you seem like a man who wouldn't want to be hampered by having...his parents around.''

The idea that she thought he was a playboy who needed his privacy was more than amusing and took the sting out of the first impression he'd taken from her question.

''Actually, I don't normally live with my parents.

I have a place of my own in the Hondo Valley. But at the moment, I'm having some remodeling done to the house. Mom and Dad's ranch house is huge, so they urged me to stay with them until the work is finished. And it's nice to spend a little time at home.''

"I'm sure," she murmured, then wondered if Adam knew what a precious thing a *home* really was. Had he ever known what it was like to be well and truly alone in the world? No. She didn't think so. She figured the most Adam Sanders ever had to worry about was where to get his expensive shirts laundered or the color to choose for his next new vehicle.

Not that Maureen resented the man's wealth. Since she'd acquired her master's degree in geology, she'd made a powerful salary. She could buy herself most anything she wanted. Yet she couldn't buy what Adam had. No one could.

"Do you have siblings?" she asked him.

He nodded. "I have a twin sister, Anna. She got married a few weeks ago to the foreman on our ranch. She and Miguel live on the property, too. Then we have a younger sister, Ivy. She's currently in medical school at the University of New Mexico." He sipped his coffee, then casually studied her over the rim of the takeout cup. "What about you, Ms. York? Do you have parents or siblings?"

Maureen's gaze dropped to the half-eaten Danish in her hand. She'd been asked this question many times in the past. Normally, it never bothered her to answer. But this morning with Adam's green eyes waiting, she'd rather have her hand chopped off.

"First of all, I told you not to call me Ms. York."

The tips of his fingers unconsciously tapped the tabletop. The movement drew Maureen's gaze to his hands. They were strong and square shaped, the backs sprinkled with dark hair. Faint scratch marks marred three of his knuckles, and from what she could see of his fingers, they were padded with calluses. He was a man who worked with his brain, but he obviously wasn't afraid to use his hands, too. She liked that about him. Liked it too much.

"All right. Maureen. Tell me about your family."

"I have no family," she said bluntly, then took a bite of the Danish as if that was all there was to say.

His brows arched upward in a you've-got-to-be-kidding expression. "Surely you have an aunt or uncle or something somewhere. What happened to your parents?"

Still avoiding his eyes, she said, "They were killed in a storm. We lived in a rural area of Texas where the nearest clinic was thirty miles away. My mother was expecting another baby any day, and thinking she'd gone into labor they decided they had no choice but to go to a doctor. The rain was blinding and part of the highway was flooded. Unseeing, they drove into the water and the swift current carried them away. I was four at the time."

She recited the story in a flat, factual voice as though she was talking about someone she hadn't known. But then it quickly struck Adam that she'd been little more than a baby when her parents had died. She hadn't known them in the sense he or any average person would know their parents.

"You were their only child?"

She nodded. "I went to live with my maternal grandmother after that. She was the only relative around who was willing to take me in. But she was elderly and she died by the time I was eight."

"What happened then?"

She looked at him, her lips compressed to a thin, mocking line. "Foster homes."

"I'm sorry," he said, the shock of her story robbing him of a better response.

"Don't be. I managed to grow up in spite of it all." She rose to her feet and crossed the room to a small trash can. After tossing in the half-eaten Danish and last dregs of her coffee, she turned back to him. "Well, I don't know what you plan to do with the rest of your day, but I'm going to get to work on these charts."

She'd lost her family, and if she had any distant relatives left, they obviously weren't the kind you counted, he mused. It was difficult to imagine what growing up in that sort of environment had been like for her. He'd had two loving parents, aunts and uncles who adored him and two sisters who'd always put him up on a pedestal. He couldn't imagine his life without any of them. And though she was trying to give him the impression that none of it had affected her that much, he knew better.

"I have plenty to do," he said, then rose to his feet and followed her back over to the cabinet where she picked up the stack of seismographic charts. "But there is something I wanted to discuss with you before I go back to my office."

In an effort to still the trembling in her hands, she gripped the graphed papers with their squiggly lines. She didn't know why it had shaken her to speak to Adam about her past. After all, lots of people had lost their parents when they were young. Lots of people had grown up in foster homes. It wasn't anything unusual or something to be ashamed of. But for some reason there was a lump as big as a fist in her throat.

"What did you want to speak to me about?" She forced her gaze to lift to his, then inwardly sighed with relief when she didn't find pity or distaste in his eyes. More than anything, she wanted Adam Sanders to see her as a strong, successful woman. A woman who'd made it on her own and was proud of her accomplishments.

"Where are you staying? Here in town?"

She nodded and named the motel. "Why do you ask?"

Adam's eyes drifted to her mouth. It was full and moist, the color of a strawberry when it turned juicy and ready to eat. The thought had him inwardly groaning with self-disgust. "I, uh, I just wanted to say there's no need for you to stay in a motel. We have plenty of room out at the ranch."

She drew in a deep breath, then let it out slowly. "Is this invitation from you or your parents?"

It was on the tip of his tongue to admit he'd first objected to the idea, but he quickly squashed it. Maybe Maureen York wasn't the cool, self-assured woman he'd originally thought. Maybe he'd let her success as a scientist cloud the picture he'd envisioned of her. She might actually need another human being from time to time. And he wouldn't be adverse to helping her if she would truly appreciate it. And him.

"Actually, the invitation is from all of us, and I told my parents I'd speak to you about it today."

Without making any sort of reply, she turned and moved away from him. The gold-framed glasses dangled from her fingers as she mulled over his suggestion.

Adam jammed his hands into the back pockets of his jeans and tried not to stare at the tall, shapely line of her figure from behind. He didn't understand his reaction to this woman. He'd had plenty of girlfriends in the past, and if someone asked him what his taste in women ran to, he'd have to say petite and delicate. The sort who looked as if the slightest squeeze from a man's hand would crush their bones. He normally loved blond hair and had always had a penchant for blue eyes. Soft and delicate and needy. Those were the things he'd always looked for in a woman. Those were the things his Susan had been made of.

But Maureen York was none of those things. She was tall with a full, ripe figure that was a far cry from delicate. She wasn't even close to being thin. She was downright curvy. Her hair and eyes were both dark. And she was at least three or four years older than him. An older woman had never turned his head before. But God help him, she was the sexiest female he'd ever encountered.

"Look, Maureen, it's not that difficult a question. You either want to stay in a boring motel room or you want to come out to the ranch. Which will it be?"

She glanced over her shoulder at him. A scowl wrinkled her brow. "I don't want to be a problem for any of you."

He shrugged as though her presence around the place would be insignificant. "The Bar M has hundreds of cattle and two barns full of horses. One more mouth to feed won't put us out."

"You really know how to…make a woman feel wanted."

A smug smile dimpled one of his cheeks. "I've been told that before."

"Oh, I'm sure you have," she replied dryly, then walked back to where he stood. "Tell your parents I really appreciate their thoughtfulness, but I—"

"What about *my* thoughtfulness?"

She cast him a doubtful frown. "Somehow I really don't believe you want me in your home."

"It's my parents' home," he reminded her. "I just happen to be staying there, too, for the time being. Besides, I invited you, didn't I?"

She shrugged. "Yes. But you also accused me of trying to kill you."

"I can forget about that if you can."

By nature, Maureen was a forgiving person. She'd never been one to harbor grudges, and even though Adam had said plenty of things to anger her, she wouldn't continue to hold it against him. No, forgetting their past quarrel would be easy. It was the other things the man did to her that had Maureen worried. Spending more time around him than was necessary would be deliberately asking for trouble.

"As far as I'm concerned, our first meeting is over and forgotten. I'm sorry you were hurt and I can understand and forgive your anger toward me."

Her head was tilted downward, her eyes veiled by thick, dark lashes. He took advantage of the unguarded moment to feast his eyes on her smooth skin. Beneath the golden tan, a faint dusting of freckles sprinkled the bridge of her nose and the ridge of her cheekbones.

Adam had the strongest urge to lean forward and press his lips to her cheeks and nose, to taste each little brown fleck. "I'm not angry anymore."

The huskiness of his voice lifted her eyes to his, and in that moment Maureen knew he was seeing her not as a co-worker, but as a woman. The idea was both terrifying and thrilling.

She nervously moistened her lips with the tip of her tongue. "I'm glad. But I'm still not sure...."

"How are you moving your things up from Houston? Or have you already?"

She shook her head. "I sold some of my furniture. What's left I'm going to have shipped with my clothes, household goods and other items in a moving van. As soon as the paperwork on the house is finalized," she added.

His expression turned incredulous. "The house! You mean you've already bought a house?"

Maureen refused to be chagrined. "Yes. I found one yesterday. Of course, it'll be at least a couple of weeks before the abstract can be read by a lawyer and everything can be signed."

"All I can say is, you don't waste time, lady."

She'd wasted...no, she swiftly corrected herself, she'd *lost* the past ten years of her life. She hadn't wasted them. But things were going to be different now. Last night, she'd vowed to put her ex-husband and their dead baby behind her once and for all. She was going to move into her new house, focus on building herself a different life and forgetting everything that she'd lost.

"I can't afford to waste time."

One brow arched curiously at her remark. "You have a date to keep?"

Her face grew stiff and devoid of emotion. "I don't have dates."

His slow perusal of her brought a tinge of color to

her cheeks. Adam didn't let her discomfiture stop him. "You'll probably think I'm impertinent," he said. "But I'm going to ask why anyway."

She turned her head away, but not before Adam spotted the faintest tremble at the corner of her lips. "You *are* being impertinent, and my personal life— or lack of one—is none of your business."

Yesterday, her clipped words would have put a smug smile on his face. He would have found enjoyment in the knowledge that she could be wounded. But today, all he could feel was an overwhelming urge to reach out and touch her.

"You're right," he said quietly, then cleared his throat and jammed his hands into the back pockets of his jeans. "It is none of my business. So let's get back to the initial question. Would you like to come stay at the ranch?"

She glanced at him, and for a split second he saw a flash of raw hunger in her eyes. The brief sight of it stabbed him right in the breastbone.

"It is tempting. I hate motel rooms."

Latching onto the uncertainty in her voice, he said, "The Bar M is beautiful. We have a swimming pool, there's always plenty of good food to eat, and you'd have a room off to yourself. You wouldn't have to see me or anyone else, unless you wanted to."

She did want to see him. That was the whole problem. But it wasn't as if she was going to throw herself into Adam Sanders's arms. Since David had walked out on her, she'd developed a willpower as strong as steel. She could resist any man.

"You make it sound very appealing." She looked at him with sudden resolution. "I think I'll accept your invitation, Adam."

He didn't know which pleased him more—her calling him by his first name or the fact that he'd won her over and she was going to be staying on the ranch.

Resisting the urge to grab her hand and smother the back of it with kisses, he said, "Good. After work this evening, I'll help you get your things from the motel and then you can follow me home."

Follow me home.

As Maureen watched him leave the lab, she tried her best not to take his words literally. This brief stay on the Bar M with Adam and his family would only be a glimpse of what she would never have.

The more she reminded herself of that fact, the safer her heart would be.

Chapter Three

Adam glanced in his rearview mirror. She was back there. Just as she'd been when he'd checked five minutes ago.

He'd really done it this time! What the hell had he been thinking? It would have made much more sense to simply reimburse Maureen for her motel expenses instead of inviting her to the ranch.

But that was the whole problem, he argued with himself. The Bar M was only his temporary home. He had to consider his parents' feelings in the matter. And he knew how pleased they would be that he'd been able to persuade Maureen to stay the next few weeks with them.

Chloe and Wyatt had always been generous people. Not just with their money or the things it could afford them to give, but generous of themselves. Adam had long wished he possessed at least a fraction of their generosity.

But now as Maureen followed him closely up the

pine-lined lane to the ranch, he wished when he'd looked into Maureen's warm brown eyes this morning, he'd been a bit stingier with his hospitality. In spite of the physical attraction he felt for her, he didn't want to get involved with her. Or any woman. And he was going to make damn sure he didn't.

Circling behind the house, Maureen parked beside Adam's truck, then joined him at the back of the vehicles. Shading her eyes from the late-evening glare, she took in the massive barns and cattle lots, the long white stables and the blue-green mountains rising up behind it all.

"When you said ranch, I didn't realize you meant a place of this magnitude," she told him, her voice filled with awe.

His wry grin was full of pride as he pulled down the tailgate on Maureen's pickup. "I told you it was beautiful."

"That's an understatement. But I didn't expect it to be a…" She paused to wave a hand at the corrals where wranglers were spreading feed into long metal troughs for a herd of steers. "A working ranch."

"Is there any other kind?"

She reached for two of her smaller cases. Adam jammed a duffel bag under one arm, then picked up two larger cases.

"Some people buy a house on an acre of land in the country and call it a ranch."

He chuckled. "We measure the Bar M in sections rather than acres."

"You sound like a genuine Texan now."

"Well, the states do touch," he said, excusing his comment.

She laughed, and Adam realized it was the first

time he'd heard the warm, rich sound or even seen her truly smile, for that matter. He thought he'd noticed everything about this woman. He'd thought her cool aloofness was because of her dislike of him. But he was beginning to think that wasn't the case at all. It wasn't him she was unhappy with. It was something inside her. Something she'd carried with her from Houston.

A man? he wondered, then groaned mockingly to himself. With a woman who looked like Maureen? Of course it was a man. And Adam hated him already.

Tossing the book onto the nightstand, Adam flopped back against the headboard and sighed. He didn't want to read. Watching TV was no option at all. Neither was lying on the bed staring at the ceiling.

Absently, he rubbed a hand over his naked chest as his gaze drifted toward the door of his bedroom. Of all the rooms in this house, his mother had insisted on putting Maureen directly across the hall from him.

Whether she'd done it on purpose or not made little difference to Adam. He'd reasoned the whole thing out with himself. He was going to be polite and hospitable to Maureen. But he was also going to be very careful about keeping his distance. Why put himself through any more temptation than he had to?

Restlessly, he rose from the bed and walked over to a pair of sliding glass doors leading out to the courtyard. A few yards away, the water in the pool glistened beneath the moonlight. He'd forgone his swim tonight. The idea of parading around in a pair of swim trunks in front of Maureen wasn't all that appealing to him. Besides, if he'd gotten into the pool earlier, his parents would surely have insisted on Maureen joining him.

Coward. Are you a man or a mouse?

The self-directed question brought a grim twist to Adam's lips. Whenever Maureen was near him, he was all too aware of which creature he was.

So what was the matter with him? It wasn't like him to run from a female. He loved women. Loved everything about them. Their softness and sweetness. Their scents and sighs and smiles.

He knew he had the reputation of a philanderer. But not one of his friends or his family really understood that deep down he was a one-woman man. And because he'd lost his one woman at the tender age of twenty-two, he refused to consider he might actually be able to find another.

Losing Susan had taught him that serious love could only lead to pain and loss. From then on, he'd closed his heart and decided that women were to be taken often and lightly.

In the last two years of college, he'd studied the female anatomy as much as he'd studied engineering, and he'd enjoyed every minute of it. But the older Adam had gotten, the stickier each relationship had become. He wanted no strings—whereas women wanted to tie him down with a damn lariat. And when they couldn't, there was always a flood of tears, the you-don't-love-me thrown in his face.

Hell! Of course he hadn't loved any of them. Where did they get the idea a little shared time and a few kisses meant a man was in love? As far as he was concerned, real love, the kind his parents shared, was very rare and even more difficult to keep. He'd lost his chance at real love when Susan's car had skidded off a rain-slick mountain highway. At this point in his life, he simply wanted to concentrate on his career.

But if he was so sure of all of that, why was he hiding in his room? he asked himself. Why didn't he simply be the Adam Murdock Sanders he'd always been, the one who wasn't afraid to enjoy and appreciate a woman's company and to hell with their tears?

Slowly, a sly smile spread across his face, then he turned away from the glass doors and went in search of his swimming trunks.

Maureen was flipping through the channels on a small television in her bedroom when a soft knock sounded on the door. She quickly pushed the Off button on the remote and reached for her dressing gown.

"Just a moment," she called.

Before opening the door, she tightened the sash at her waist and adjusted the overlap of material between her breast. A second later, she was glad she'd taken the time to cover herself. Adam was standing on the threshold with nothing on but a pair of swimming trunks and a devilish smile.

"How about a swim?"

Incredulous, she stared at him. "A swim?"

He put a shushing finger to his lips. "Yes. A swim. You know, me and you in the water. Staying afloat, cooling off."

Maureen had to stifle the mocking burst of laughter rising up her throat. Cool off with Adam? She didn't think so.

"It's nearly time for bed," she reasoned.

He glanced at the moon just then bursting over the ridge of mountains to the east. "This is the best time of the day. Not too hot. Not too cool. And don't worry, the moonlight isn't bright enough to show off your cellulite.''

Her narrowed eyes warned him he was treading on dangerous ground. "What makes you think I have cellulite?''

A grin kept trying to tug at the corners of his mouth. It would have infuriated her on any other man. On Adam, she wanted to lean forward and taste it.

"Nothing. I just know how you women worry about such trivial things.''

Her brows arched at the word *trivial*. "So you don't mind if a woman has a few flaws?''

The grin appeared in full force as he shook his head. "No. I turn a blind eye to them. After all, a perfect woman would be...boring. If you ask me,'' he added.

Maureen wished she hadn't asked. She also wished he wasn't looking at her as though he'd like to slip the blue cotton robe off her shoulders, then eat her for dessert.

"I guess we women are lucky there's no perfect men around to...bore us.''

Adam chuckled. "So are you coming with me or not?''

She spared him one last look before glancing over her shoulder at the bed. She wasn't ready for sleep. Certainly not now after he'd stirred her hormones to a heady boil. But was she ready for a moonlight swim with Adam?

"It's dangerous to swim alone,'' he persisted.

"How do you know I can even swim?'' she countered.

His gaze traveled lazily down the length of her.

"You don't look like you'd have any problem with the sport."

The only problem she had was with him. Maybe it was time she showed him she was not a woman to be flirted with. Not by him or any man.

"I don't. So give me a couple of minutes to change and I'll meet you out in the courtyard," she told him.

When Maureen appeared a few minutes later on the patio, Adam was stretched out on a chaise lounge. A tall pitcher of some sort of fruity-looking drink sat beside him on a low table. The two iced glasses next to it told Maureen he had been busy while she changed into her swimsuit.

"What's that?" she asked, inclining her head toward the pink drink.

"Some of my aunt Rose's special punch. She knows how much I like it, so whenever she makes a batch, she brings some by the ranch for me."

"Do all the women around here spoil you?" Maureen slipped off her short cover-up and sat on the chaise next to Adam. Immediately, she could feel his eyes all over her loose hair and bare skin.

"Spoil me? What makes you think that?"

She made a sound of disbelief. "Your mother cooks you *chorizo* and eggs every morning. Your aunt makes you a special punch. That sounds like spoiling to me."

Grinning, Adam leaned over in the chair, then poured both glasses full of punch. "What can I say? I'm a loved man."

What must that feel like? Maureen wondered. After her grandmother died, there'd been no one to coddle or cluck over her. Just a list of foster parents who'd seen to her physical needs but hadn't come close to meeting the emotional void left by her parents' and grandmother's deaths. She supposed that was the reason she'd clung to David for so long after their baby daughter had succumbed to crib death. She'd been devastated and desperately needed her husband's love to help her get past the loss of her baby. But his love, if he'd ever had any for her, had stopped after little Elizabeth had died. He'd blamed her for the death, then walked out on her.

Mentally shaking away the black memories, Maureen accepted the proffered glass from Adam's hand and took a careful sip. The concoction had the consistency of a milk shake. It tasted of strawberries and pineapple with a heavy dose of banana. "This is sinfully rich."

"And very good."

"And very good," she agreed.

Several moments passed as they drank in silence. All the while, Maureen could feel his eyes studying her as though she were a test paper and he was trying to figure out the answers.

Placing her glass on the low table, she looked at him. "Have you found any yet?"

His forehead wrinkled with confusion. "Excuse me?"

"Cellulite. Do I have any? Or should I stand and let you inspect the back half of me?"

He didn't appear to be the least bit embarrassed. Amused was more like it.

"You look...different without your clothes." And oddly enough, he decided seeing her hair free from its braid and rippling to her hips was just as intimate a view as the upper swells of her beautiful bosom.

"Most of us do," she said dryly.

Different was not the description he was actually thinking. Luscious was much closer. Her swimsuit was a white one piece with high-cut legs and a low-cut neck that showed a generous amount of cleavage. Her body was the same golden tan as her face. The image of a toasted marshmallow drifted into his mind and he wondered if the inside of her would be as soft and sweet.

"You still don't like me much, do you?"

His question had her reaching for her drink. She swallowed down a sip before she answered. "You're not bad. For a company man."

She couldn't know how much Adam disliked that term. True, he was technically what people in the oil and gas business called "a company man." But he knew a roughneck or driller or tool pusher classified him in the same loathsome way a private did his drill sergeant. Adam wasn't a man who necessarily needed or wanted that much authority. But it was something that went with the job.

"What made you want to be a geologist?" he asked curiously.

Leaning back in the chaise, she stretched her long legs out in front of her. The night air was balmy. Adam had been right. This was the best time of the day.

"Ever since I was a little girl, I wanted to know why. Why was the grass green? Why did the stars shine? Why did sodium bicarbonate make buttermilk bubble? I looked forward to science class the way other girls eagerly awaited a Friday-night date."

One corner of his lips curved with wry amusement. "Don't tell me you didn't look forward to those Friday-night dates."

She drew in a deep breath and stared at the raspberry polish on her toenails. "Not really."

"You must have dated sometime. You were married."

She looked at him in surprise. "How did you know that?"

He shrugged. "Down in South America. Remember? You told me you were divorced."

She'd remembered, but she'd figured the most he recalled about their first meeting was the accident. "Well, I didn't date until I was a freshman in college," she explained. "That's when I met David. After a year we were married. Another year later we were divorced."

"What happened?"

She frowned at him. "What do you mean, what happened?"

"The divorce. Something obviously came between the two of you. What was it, another woman?"

If only it had been that simple, Maureen thought. She might have been able to deal with a cheating husband. As it was, she'd struggled to hang on to a man who'd viewed her as a selfish woman and a negligent mother. Looking back on it now, she seriously doubted David had ever felt more than physical lust for her.

"No. David didn't have a roaming eye for other women. After we were married, I..." She sighed and shook her head against the dark memories. "I discovered we had totally different objectives in life."

"Such as?"

Her frown deepened. "Don't you think you're getting a bit personal?"

He shrugged and put his drink aside, then swung

his legs over the side of the chair to face her. With his elbows resting on his knees, he leaned forward and studied her thoughtfully. "Not personal. Just curious as to why any man would let you go."

Something soft and uniquely feminine flickered deep inside her. Something she hadn't felt in years. "You make me sound like a prize," she said, a thread of accusation in her husky voice.

The only change in his expression was a faint arch to his brows. "Most women would consider being called a prize a compliment. Obviously, you didn't take it that way."

He was making her edgy and restless and a little more than confused. For years she'd told herself she would never let herself belong to another man. Being David's prize had taken everything from her. Her pride and self-respect, even a certain degree of the ambition she'd always possessed. And then there were all those years she'd struggled to shed herself of the guilt he'd instilled in her. No, she didn't want to be another man's prize.

But the woman in her, that foolish, needy feminine part, wondered what it would be like to belong to Adam Murdock Sanders. To have him make love to her as though she was his and only his.

The disturbing thought pushed Maureen to her feet. A glance at his face told her he was still waiting for her reply. "I'm a person," she said simply. "A human being. Not a prize to be possessed."

She walked away from him and stood at the edge of the pool. She was staring down into its cool depths when she heard his footfall behind her, and then his hand was on her bare shoulder, sending tingling little shots of fire over her skin.

"Is that what happened with your husband?" he asked quietly.

"Don't say husband," she said flatly. "David is a very *ex*-husband. I haven't seen him for more than ten years."

Suddenly, she turned to face him. The movement caused his hand to slip to her upper arm. Unconsciously, his fingers moved ever so slightly against her skin.

"Why are we talking about this? We're supposed to be swimming. You know, me and you in the water. Staying afloat. Cooling off," she said, using the same words he'd used on her earlier.

She was comfortable with letting him see the outside of her, but not the inside. Not the part of her that really mattered. Adam told himself that was all well and good. He didn't need to know Maureen's hopes and dreams, past or future. Light and casual. That was the best way, the only way, for him to deal with Maureen York.

Slowly, a glint appeared in his eyes. The sight of it flashed a warning to Maureen, but she was too slow in reacting. Before she could step away, Adam's hands were gripping the sides of her waist.

"You're right, Maureen. Let's go!"

"Adam!"

His name screeched from her lips as he jumped over the side of the pool, taking her along with him. As they plunged into the cool water, his hands remained clasped on her ribs, forcing Maureen to sink slowly to the bottom with him.

The buoyancy of the water caused their bare legs to tangle. Like magnets against steel, their bodies slammed together, and Maureen was instantly overwhelmed with the sensation of his hard body pressed against her thighs, her belly and breasts.

Frantic to escape the arousing heat rocketing through her veins, she put her hands on his shoulders and tried to shove herself away. Sensing her panic, Adam gave one hard kick to push the both of them to the surface. Their heads broke the water only inches apart. She was greedily gasping for air. He was grinning, waiting eagerly for her to explode.

Once she managed to push away the wet hair plastered over her eyes, she glared at him. "Are you crazy?"

His white teeth gleamed in the moonlight. "Depends on whom you ask."

Because they were in the deep end of the pool, they were forced to tread water to stay afloat. But somehow Adam was managing even while one hand was occupied with a hold on the side of her waist.

"Is this the way you treat all your women guests? Throw them into a freezing pool, then try to drown them?"

He chuckled with devilish amusement. "The water is plenty warm. And what makes you think I have other women guests out here?"

This time, she was the one to laugh; only it was a sound of disbelief rather than amusement. "If you hadn't noticed by now, I was born before you. Not yesterday. Don't insult my intelligence by telling me you've been living like a monk."

His head tilted back as more laughter rumbled from his throat. Maureen looked at him while thinking she had never seen a man quite as sexual as this one. And it wasn't just the pleasing shape of his features or his thick auburn hair or even his very male attitude. She wasn't quite sure what it was about him. But the faint squint of his eyes, the sensual little curve to his lips and the strong angle of his jaw all worked together to do strange things to her sleeping libido.

"I would never profess to be so holy," he admitted. "But I can safely say I've never had a female guest out here to the ranch. Not the sort you're thinking."

She continued to look at him doubtfully. Adam took her hand and used her forefinger to make the mark of a cross over his heart.

"Cross my heart," he said lowly.

"Okay. I believe you. Not that it matters. Now you can let go of me...before we both drown." She plucked her hand from his and paddled the water.

"I'm staying afloat quite nicely like this, thank you," he told her. "But if you need help..."

He didn't finish. Instead, he quickly flipped her onto her back, then supported her floating weight with one palm beneath her shoulder blade and the other against the small of her back.

"Adam, let me loose!"

She tried to backstroke away from him, but he snagged a thumb beneath the edge of her suit and held tight. "I will," he promised huskily. "In a minute. Just relax and look up at the stars."

The moon had risen far above the mountaintops now, and his face was cast in silvery light and shadows. The impish curl to his lips implied he was merely playing, but the droop of his eyelids said there was another part of him that earnestly wanted to seduce her.

"And what are you going to look at?" she asked him.

"You."

His blatant answer sent a little shiver down her spine. Adam must have felt her reaction because he guided her body closer so the side of her waist was curved against his chest.

"You really are cold, aren't you?"

Cold? She very nearly laughed. How could she be cold when his body heat was surging through her like a hot bolt of electricity?

"No. And I didn't come out here for you to manhandle me," she said with as much primness as she could muster.

He shot her an innocent look. "I'm not manhandling you."

"Well, you're not exactly letting me go, either."

His eyelids drooped lower as his gaze scanned her moonlit face. "I don't want to let you go."

That was the last thing she expected him to say and her lips parted with surprise. What was he doing? Trying to ruin their working relationship before it ever really started?

She turned her head toward him, and her long hair floated against his arm like a piece of gossamer silk. "Are you trying to scare me away from Sanders?"

He stared at her. "Scare you?"

The dumbfounded look on his face answered her question. Scaring her was the very last thing on his mind, and she didn't know if she felt relief or a deep-seated fear.

"Maureen, if I really didn't want you working at Sanders, there'd be other ways to get rid of you. I wouldn't do it by half drowning you in a pool."

That wasn't the sort of scaring she meant. But it was fine with her if that was where his thinking lay.

Besides, she was drowning. In him. And the whole idea terrified her. Still, she wasn't about to let him know just how strongly he was affecting her. She'd joined him tonight with every intention of giving him a lesson in older women. She had to carry it off.

"Then what *are* you doing?" she asked in as level a voice as she could manage.

"Enjoying the moonlight and the water. And you."

She expected him to add a grin to his words. When he didn't, she fought off a shiver and tried to block out the feel of his hands on her back and the bulge of his chest muscles pressing against her side.

"You know, when I first met you, I thought you were a stuffed shirt. Now I have to rearrange my impressions. You're really a...rascal in wolf's clothing."

His mouth quirked with amusement. "I'm not wearing much clothing at the moment," he pointed out.

Did he think she needed to be reminded of that fact? "Yesterday you couldn't stand the sight of me. Tonight I can't get you to take your hands off me. Are you always this capricious?"

Adam had never been an unpredictable man. Once he had his mind set, it was nigh impossible for anyone to change it. What Maureen didn't know was that he'd wanted to touch her just as badly yesterday as he did at this moment. And the whole idea annoyed the hell out of him.

"I thought we'd put all those hard feelings behind us."

A laugh of disbelief slipped from her throat. "So we did. But do you think that gives you the right to...take liberties?"

The corner of his mouth tilted upward at her use of the old-fashioned expression. "Maureen, I'm not taking liberties. I thought we were just having a swim. And a little…fun."

Fun. His sort of fun was not Maureen's taste in amusement. Not when she knew how much pain it could eventually wreak on a woman's state of mind. Not to mention her heart.

With sudden decisiveness, she raised her head and moved so close her face was only a few inches from his. "So you want to play, huh?" she murmured throatily, then lifting her hand, she thrust it into his wet hair and scraped it back against his sleek skull.

Bemused by her abrupt switch, Adam could only stare at the gleam in her dark eyes, at the drops of water on her cheeks and the moisture clinging to her rose-colored lips.

"What—what are you doing?" he stammered.

One corner of her lips moved into a half smile and her teeth glinted brightly against her shadowed face. "Giving you what you want."

Before he could ask more, she leaned forward until her face became a blur and then, unbelievably, her lips were pressed to his. Warm, open and searching.

Too stunned to do much at all, Adam could only clutch her waist. Their lips fused together, then slowly they drifted in the water until Adam's back bumped into the wall of the pool. By this point his shocked senses were wide-awake and he groaned with disappointment when the heated velvet of her lips lifted away from his.

"Was that supposed to be some sort of lesson?" he asked huskily.

She studied him beneath lowered eyelids. "Yes. A

lesson that I'm not to be toyed with. I'm not one of those young girls that you toss away like a faded rose."

His eyes widened ever so slightly. "Where did you hear something like that?"

She smiled mockingly but still didn't move away. Adam wondered if she was deliberately trying to torture him with her hand curved intimately against his neck, the front of her body brushing against his, teasing him with erotic images.

"I heard a couple of the secretaries talking about the last dish you threw away. They were pestered with her calls for weeks afterward."

He scowled. Maureen made it sound as though he was a user. And that had never been the case with Adam. He'd never given any woman false promises. He'd never pledged love or happily-ever-after.

"The woman wouldn't accept that I wasn't serious."

Maureen's features hardened. "Well, I *am* serious. So don't mess with me."

Her hands-off warning was like fuel to his already smoldering senses. When she started to turn away from him, Adam grabbed her chin and held it fast.

"And what would you do if I told you I *was* serious?" he asked in a husky growl. "What would you do if I told you that at this very moment I want you more than I've ever wanted any woman?"

Her nostrils flared and her breast heaved. "I'd say you were using one of your well-practiced lines on me."

A strangled sound erupted from his throat, and then he was jerking her forward, planting his lips over hers.

Like the instant detonation of a bomb, heat erupted inside her. It spread to every finger and toe and seared the roots of her hair. Kissing him of her own volition was one thing. But now he'd turned the tables and she was withering, clinging helplessly to the erotic magic his lips were creating on hers.

The slow yielding of her body and the parting of her lips were all the silent invitation Adam needed. He crushed her closer and thrust his tongue between her teeth.

A tiny moan sounded in Maureen's throat, and then Adam felt the two of them slowly sinking, drowning in each other and the water. Only the burning need for oxygen forced them to break free and kick to the surface. Maureen seized the moment to escape from him and swim across the pool.

As she climbed the ladder and stepped out onto the tile, Adam called to her. "Where are you going?"

Unable to look at him, she continued making her way toward the house. "In. Before you drown the both of us!"

Adam watched her go, her long, wet hair swaying to the rhythm of her hips. Desire, hot and fierce, throbbed inside him, and he had to concede that she'd been right. She wasn't like any of the young women he'd flirted and dallied with in the past. She was something else altogether. And he needed to keep his hands off before she burned them and a few other pieces of his anatomy to a crisp.

But even with the warning echoing in his head, it was all Adam could do to keep from climbing out of the pool and going after her.

Chapter Four

The next morning, Maureen declined Chloe's invitation to join the family for breakfast. Instead, she had coffee in her room, then stopped on her way to work and picked up a couple of pastries.

She realized avoiding breakfast with the Sanderses was cowardly of her. But after what took place between her and Adam in the pool the night before, she hadn't been ready to face him across the dining table.

Thoughts of being in his strong arms, kissing his hard lips, still had the power to curl her toes. She knew she was running scared, but she couldn't help herself. Since David had been out of her life, no man had turned her head. No man had even gotten close enough to touch her in an intimate way. So what on earth had possessed her to kiss Adam as though she was some sort of wanton hussy?

The question had her groaning as she entered the small laboratory at the back of the Sanders building. She didn't know what had come over her. But she was certain of one thing; she wasn't going to let it happen again.

And with that determined thought, she went to the filing cabinets and pulled out the work she'd started yesterday.

Adam placed the telephone back on its cradle, then let out a long sigh. He'd been at work two hours. So far, he'd been too tied up with important calls to head back to the lab to see Maureen. Which was probably all for the best. He didn't have a clue as to what to say to her. He wasn't even sure he should bring up their... well, whatever it was that had happened between the two of them last night.

Leaning back in the big leather chair, Adam scraped his fingers through the lank of hair pestering his brow. Dear heaven, he'd never had any woman set him on fire as she had. And he refused to think what might have happened if she hadn't put a halt to things.

He couldn't have an affair with Maureen York. He had to work with the woman! With that thought in mind, he left his office and headed for the lab.

When footsteps passed near the back of her chair, Maureen was hunched over her work and deep in thought. Thinking it was one of the men with soil samples, she didn't bother glancing over her shoulder.

"If they're labeled, just put them anywhere," she said. "I'll find them."

"I'm not the delivery boy."

The sound of his voice jerked Maureen's head up and around. With her heart going like a jackhammer in her chest, it was hard to keep her expression cool as she looked at him, but she managed it somehow.

"Good morning, Adam. Is there something I can do for you?"

He silently groaned. She was being cool and professional, and all he could think about was tossing her down on the worktable and ravishing every inch of her. Well, if she could act as though nothing had ever happened between them, then Adam could, too.

He folded his arms against his chest. "Maybe. I need to know something definite about well fifty-five. Have you had a chance to look over the information I gave you on it yesterday?"

Nodding, she rose to her feet and carefully stepped around him. Across the room, she picked up a manila folder from a cabinet counter and carried it back to where he stood.

"It's all in here. I've studied everything thoroughly and my advice to you is to forget the whole thing."

"Forget it? Are you mad? Do you realize how much money Sanders has sunk into that hole? We need to reach that gas and *you're* the one who's supposed to know how to do it."

Her brows arched and her shoulders straightened to an even more rigid line. Maureen might be uncertain of herself as a woman but not as a geologist.

"I'm very aware of how much money the company's already spent on fifty-five. It's right here in the report. That's one of the reasons I'm advising against drilling in at another angle. There just isn't enough gas there to warrant the expense."

Adam was hearing every word she was saying, and even though a part of his mind was registering her opinion, the other part was shocked at how much he simply wanted to touch her, taste her.

"Our last geologist assured us there was plenty of gas to be found along that particular mountain ridge."

Her smile was anything but warm. "Maybe that's why he doesn't work here anymore."

Adam's nostrils flared as he fought with not only what she was telling him, but also his desire to reach out and clamp his hand around her chin and drag her lips up to his.

"Show me," he clipped.

She stared at him. "Show you what?"

Frustration tightened his features. "How you can be so certain of all this."

"It's a scientific deduction. Even if I laid it all out in front of you, I don't think you'd understand."

That jolted him, and the smile that suddenly exposed his straight white teeth was a dare in itself.

"Really?"

She grimaced at his cockiness. "I thought you were an engineer."

"I am. But I have another degree in geophysics."

Maureen unconsciously gripped the manila folder as she studied his smug face. It didn't bother her that he was also a scientist. In fact, she admired him for acquiring the knowledge. It was the personal side of him that was making her grit her teeth and wonder why she'd ever agreed to this job. She couldn't let last night repeat itself. She couldn't let this crazy attraction she had for this man get out of control.

"Then why did your father bother hiring me?" she asked.

His answering grin was as phony as the sweetness in her voice. "Because I'm not nearly as qualified as you are...in the geology field. Besides, I'm needed as a company man."

Maureen stepped past him and marched over to the long worktable sitting in the middle of the room. As she laid out the contents of the folders, she said, "I can certainly understand that. You have the perfect attitude for it."

He sauntered over to the table and stopped a step away from her left shoulder. "What is that supposed to mean?" he asked.

To look at him was like being given a dose of heaven and hell, so she kept her gaze on the tabletop. "Your father could search several states and not find anyone with your brashness."

If she was trying to get his hackles up, she was succeeding wonderfully, Adam thought as he tried to unclamp his jaw. "It's a necessary trait. In case you're not aware of it, rig workers are usually a rough breed of men."

From the corner of her eye, she slanted him a mocking glance. "You wouldn't have a gas and oil company without them."

He made a sound of disgust. "I know that better than anyone. And don't think I take their hard work for granted. It's just that you can't treat them the same way you would a group of ballet dancers."

"In other words, they have to know you're even tougher than they are."

He inclined his head toward her. "That's about the size of it. If they don't fear me enough to take pride in their work, then we have a problem."

Well, Maureen could admit to herself that she feared Adam Murdock Sanders. Not where her job was concerned, but in the matter of her heart, where she could be hurt the very most.

Releasing a long breath, she turned her attention

back to the papers she'd lined meticulously on the tabletop and tapped her forefinger against one of the seismograph tests. "This is enough to tell me there's very little gas there. And this—" she pointed to the paper lying next in line "—tells me you'd have to drill through a great depth of rock to get to it. And this—"

Her words broke off as his hand suddenly came down over hers, and her shocked gaze flew up to his face.

"What are you doing?" she demanded. "If you think I'm going to play office games with you, you're very much mistaken. I realize last night—"

"Damn it, Maureen, I'm not trying to play anything," he interrupted gruffly. "I'm just trying to get your attention. Your real attention."

From the moment she'd realized he was in the room, every fiber in her body had come to his attention. Thank God he didn't know that, Maureen thought miserably.

"Why?" she asked warily.

He heaved out a frustrated breath. "Because I don't like the way we are right now."

Maureen tried to still the rapid thumping of her heart, but with him standing so near, it refused to obey. She could only hope he didn't look down and see the faint movement of her shirt.

"How…are we?" she wanted to know.

He grimaced. "Treating each other like two strangers. No, I take that back. Two strangers would probably be nicer to each other."

"I don't think…" The touch of his hand on hers made it impossible for Maureen to go on. She pulled away from his grasp and turned her back to him. "I don't believe we can be nice to each other, Adam," she said quietly.

"Why? You dislike me that much?"

His question made her wince inwardly. She liked him too much. That was the whole problem. A problem she had to keep to herself.

"No. I don't dislike you. But…" She forced herself to turn back around to him. "Last night—"

"Should never have happened," he finished for her.

Her gaze dropped to his boots. Instantly, she noticed the gap he'd slit in the instep of the ostrich leather. She realized the Jeep accident had dealt him a host of miseries and she regretted that. But she had also thanked God over and over for not taking his life that day. She couldn't bear to imagine what the world would be like without this vibrant man in it.

"I agree. It was reckless and foolish behavior on my part," she said.

And she regretted it completely. He could see it all over her downcast face.

"I don't know about all that," he said, trying not to sound as deflated as he felt. "I'd say we were…well, the whole thing was dangerous more than anything else."

Dangerous. Oh, yes, Maureen thought, the kisses they'd shared had been all that and more. "You're right," she murmured.

He swallowed as the urge to reach out and touch her surged through him like an overwhelming thirst for water. "I won't let it happen again."

She ordered her head to lift. When her eyes met his, she felt a jolt right down to her toes. "Neither will I."

Adam should have been shouting with joyous relief. She wasn't blaming him for what happened. Nor was she wanting to pick up where they'd left off. Everything was fine, except that he felt hollow with disappointment. He could only hope in a few days' time the feeling would pass and he'd realize the wisdom of the pact to keep things between them impersonal.

"Then we can put this behind us?" he asked.

One corner of her lips tilted upward. "We're adults. Surely we can behave in a grown-up manner."

"We have to work together, Maureen. I don't want our time on the job to be miserable."

He was right. At times, the two of them would have to work closely together. One way or the other, they would have to get along. But how could she look at him as just a co-worker when he'd already been more? She'd just have to forget, she supposed. Forget he'd kissed her with a hunger that still had the power to burn her memory.

"Neither do I," she agreed. "And you're right. We have to—make sure last night never repeats itself."

An agreeable woman had never annoyed Adam before. But hearing Maureen calmly allow that the two of them should never lay their hands on one another again was not exactly good for his ego. Or any other part of him.

"Good," he finally managed to say. "I'm glad we've got this all settled."

In Maureen's mind, nothing was settled, but during the past ten years, she'd gotten good at pretending and hiding her true feelings. She had to do it now.

"Now, about well fifty-five," she said, determined to get back to business. "If you think my decision is wrong, just say so. I'll be glad to go over the report again. But I won't promise it will change my opinion."

He leaned over and gathered up the papers Maureen had carefully laid out for him to see. Once he had them all back inside the manila folder, he said, "That won't be necessary. I'm going to tell Dad to pull the plug."

Maureen's mouth fell open as her eyes searched his face. "But you—you were just arguing." Her mouth snapped shut and she shook her head at him. "You were questioning my judgment."

A wry grin twisted his lips. "Not really. I just wanted to see if you were really sure of yourself. You are. So I'm satisfied."

She wanted to slap his face and kick his shins until he howled in pain. Instead, her expression turned icy. "I'm so glad you're satisfied. Now if you'll excuse me, I have work to do."

Maureen didn't wait for a reply—she just turned and walked away from him. She was at the filing cabinet, pretending to search for a folder, when she heard his footsteps leaving the room. Once the door closed behind him with a soft click, she sagged against the metal drawers and let out a long breath.

Dealing with Adam Murdock Sanders was going to be much harder than she'd thought. Much harder.

"Have you eaten a bucket of nails or something?"

Adam glanced up from the saddle he was cleaning. His twin sister, Anna, was striding up the alleyway of the horse barn, tugging a reluctant sorrel yearling behind her. At the moment, the animal's ears lay pinned against his head, his nostrils were flared and the whites of his eyes were showing. Apparently, his mood wasn't any better than Adam's.

"I haven't eaten anything since lunch. What've you done to him?" he asked, nodding toward the colt.

"Nothing yet. He just knows something is about to happen and he's afraid he isn't going to like it."

Adam knew the feeling. It hit him every time he walked into the same room with Maureen York. Not that he'd had any more confrontations with the woman. Quite the contrary, in fact. Not one cross word had passed between them. Whenever the two of them had anything to discuss, she was cool, polite and professional. He should be pleased about their new-found relationship, but in truth, he despised her indifference and his phony reaction to it.

By now, Anna had reached his workplace, a little secluded area just off the tack room. Pausing, she gave her brother a puzzled frown. "What's your problem?" Anna persisted.

Adam turned his attention back to the saddle resting on the hitching rail. The task was mundane, but bringing the leather back to life was something he enjoyed. Especially when he was out of sorts and needed time to ponder things. For the past hour, he'd been asking himself why he'd not been content to be just a rancher. He loved the life. The outdoors, the livestock, the hard manual labor of it all. But something had driven him on to be an oilman just like his father. And he wondered what had driven Maureen to be a geologist. Even more, what had really called her out here to New Mexico. And him.

"I don't have one."

"It's not normal for you to come home early to

work in the stables. Your lunch must have been sour.''

"If it was sour, the acid in my stomach took care of it.''

"I don't doubt that. You must be full of the stuff.''

He jammed the polishing cloth into the back pocket of his jeans and turned to face his sister. "Are you trying to tell me I'm not the charming man I usually am?''

The redhead laughed heartily. "You look like you could commit murder. I don't know why you came down here in such a mood.''

"Where would you have me go? A bar, so I could drown the acid with alcohol?''

She made a face at him and he frowned back at her. No one knew him like his twin. The two of them had always shared a closeness that superseded the normal bonds between siblings. If Anna was hurting, he sensed it. If he was in pain, Anna knew it.

"No, I don't want you in a nasty ole bar,'' she said. The colt began to jig nervously away from her. She tugged on the lead rope and forced him back to her side. "What's the matter anyway? Are you having it out with the new geologist Daddy hired?''

Adam cocked a wary brow at her. "Having it out?''

She frowned at him. "You know what I mean. Daddy said you two had a row the first moment you laid eyes on each other.''

"Humph,'' he snorted. "We got that all straightened out. I've forgiven her for breaking my ankle.'' He just couldn't forgive her for being so beautiful, so damn tempting.

"How generous of you,'' Anna said sweetly, then

motioned for him to follow her. "I need some help with this little devil. Will you hold him while I clip his mane?"

Adam groaned. "Why do you want to get me killed?"

Anna laughed. "You look like you need to be put out of your misery. Come on."

"You're so funny," he retorted, but followed her and the horse down to the grooming pen anyway.

As expected, the yearling put up a good fight. By the time Anna turned off the clippers, Adam had been bitten, stomped and rope burned. His sister tried not to giggle at the look of disgust on her brother's face, but a few spurts of laughter managed to escape in spite of her efforts.

"I'm sorry, Adam, but I did offer to let you do the cutting while I did the holding."

He carefully peeled away the loose hide hanging from his forearm. "Don't worry about it. I'll survive."

Her giggles subsided. "Actually, it's your state of mind that's worrying me."

"Well, I apologize for not dancing around with a happy smile on my face. It's been a hard week, and I have things on my mind."

Anna thoughtfully tapped a finger against her chin. "And you're sure it has nothing to do with Maureen York?"

"Nothing," he barked.

"And it doesn't bother you that she's staying here on the ranch?"

"Hell, no! She stays in her room, and I do as I please. We don't even see each other."

Anna looked at him with wide, knowing eyes. "Oh, well, no wonder you're so grouchy."

"What is that supposed to mean?" he growled.

Anna quickly grabbed the yearling's lead rope and trotted away from her brother. "Nothing," she called cheerily over her shoulder.

"Anna, you're crazy!" he yelled back at her.

"That's better than being lonely."

Lonely? Hell, what's she talking about now? Adam grumbled to himself. Just because she was head over heels in love with her new husband didn't mean he was pining for a mate.

"I realize I'm rushing you," Maureen said to the real-estate agent, "but I need the house as quickly as possible. I'm willing to pay extra. Yes. Whatever it takes to get the papers finalized."

For the next five minutes, Maureen listened patiently to the agent's excuses and promises. By the time she hung up, she wanted to scream with frustration. It was the third time she'd called the man this week and she figured he was probably as sick of dealing with her as she was with him. But Maureen couldn't help it. She had to get away from this ranch as soon as possible.

Rising from the stuffed armchair, she walked over to the window and pushed back the heavy muslin curtain. Her room didn't have a privileged view of the courtyard but rather looked out at the distant mountain range to the north.

Which was likely for the best, Maureen thought. Each time she caught a glimpse of the shimmering swimming pool, her thoughts turned to Adam and the night they'd dived into the pool and each other.

All this past week she'd tried to put her attraction to him in proper perspective. She kept telling herself it would pass. She promised herself she was only suffering a fleeting, physical malady that would eventually cure itself. But so far, that hadn't happened. Each time Adam approached her, everything came rushing back. The kisses, the hunger, the incredible excitement she'd experienced in his arms.

For the first time in years, Maureen felt helpless and scared. She didn't want any man to have such a powerful effect on her. And to fight it, she'd done the only thing she could think of to do. She kept as much distance as possible between her and Adam. And whenever he'd been near, she'd made sure every word, every look, was cool and professional.

But the strain of acting was beginning to take its toll, and she didn't know how much more she could take. At work she could make herself struggle through the day. But knowing she had to come back to the Bar M in the evenings and face the risk of running into him each time she left her room was too much for her nerves to bear. She had to get into her own house. And fast.

Still, Maureen was sick of cowering in her room every evening like a timid little rabbit. She couldn't let Adam control her every move!

With that thought in mind, she changed out of her dirty work clothes and into clean jeans and a white, short-sleeved camp shirt. The French braid hanging down the middle of her back was ragged, so she brushed it loose and anchored her hair away from her face with a white headband. Then she left her room and headed to the kitchen.

It was still too early for supper. Chloe hadn't yet

returned to the house from the stables, much less started preparing a meal.

Content to settle for something cool to drink, Maureen poured herself a small glass of orange juice. As she sipped, she wondered why Adam's mother didn't hire a live-in cook and housekeeper. The Sanderses could certainly afford the extra help. Just their gas exploration business alone must be worth a staggering amount. Not to mention the ranch.

But from what Maureen could see, neither Chloe nor any of the family lived as if they had money to burn. Including Adam. The only extravagant thing she'd noticed about him was his ostrich boots, and since he'd taken his pocketknife to one of them, they were hardly anything to flaunt.

A door behind her opened and closed. Maureen turned away from the refrigerator just in time to see Adam entering the kitchen. Her fingers unconsciously tightened on the glass in her hand, and her chin lifted.

"Hello, Maureen."

The softly spoken words took her by complete surprise. The two of them had already talked earlier that morning at work. Their conversation had been brief, to the point and, for the most part, agreeable. He'd greeted her coolly and she'd returned the brisk hello with an even shorter one. So what did this new greeting mean?

"Hello," she returned.

He moved into the room, and her heart hammered as her gaze slipped up and down the length of him. His faded jeans were dusty, the thighs spotted with stains. The front of his pale blue shirt was dark with sweat, while the sleeves were rolled to his elbows. A rusty shadow of beard covered his jaw and upper lip.

And as Maureen looked at him, she knew she was seeing sex appeal in its rawest form.

"Looks like you've been working," she said.

He opened a cabinet door and took down a glass. As he approached the refrigerator, Maureen moved a few steps aside.

"My mother and sister allowed me to help in the stables this evening," he said.

"Allowed?"

Seeing the curious arch to her brow, Adam knew his statement had puzzled her. "Maybe no one's bothered to explain to you that my mother and sister raise and train racehorses. And they're very picky about whom they let near them."

"Even you?"

She sounded incredulous, and he grunted with dry amusement. "Yeah. Even me."

"Aren't you a horseman?"

He filled his glass with water from the door dispenser and took several long swallows before he answered. "I grew up on a horse. And I suppose I can handle one as well as the next man. But racehorses are a different matter entirely. I don't have the patience for their hot temperaments."

"I can believe that," she murmured.

He shot her a wry glance. "Surely you don't think I'm high-strung."

She took a sip of her juice, then carefully licked her lips. Adam's gaze followed the lazy movement of her tongue and he tried not to groan out loud. There was hardly a minute in the day that didn't go by without his thinking of making love to Maureen York. And he was beginning to wonder just how much time it was going to take to cure him of the mental torture.

"I think…you're always champing at the bit."

In spite of everything, Adam laughed. The sound of pleasure put a tilt to Maureen's lips, and as he looked at her, he realized this was what he'd missed with her this past week. This personal connection was what he needed most.

"It's nice to hear you speaking your mind again."

She studied him over the rim of her glass. This evening, he was wearing an old battered Stetson. The brim was rolled up on the sides and dipped low in the front. Instead of a band, the crown was circled with sweat stains. Maureen decided the reckless character of the gray hat suited him well.

"What do you mean 'again'? I always speak my mind."

"Not with me."

She studied him guardedly. "I tell you exactly what I think."

"Yes. About work."

She needed air, but her lungs unexpectedly refused to work. "Is there anything else…but work?"

He leaned over and placed his glass on a nearby counter, then took a few steps closer to her. Maureen forced herself to breathe deeply and keep her feet rooted to the floor.

"Look, Maureen, I know…" He shook his head, then folded his arms across his chest.

At that moment, Maureen caught a glimpse of his forearm, and it suddenly didn't matter what he'd been about to say. She gasped audibly. "Adam! What have you done to yourself?" Before he could answer, she rushed forward and took hold of his arm.

Her closeness, the touch of her soft hands, was

worth the searing pain of the rope burn, he decided. Then cursed himself for being such a fool.

"It's nothing, Maureen. A yearling got a little rowdy, that's all."

"Nothing! This is plowed flesh. And..." She stopped speaking as she bent her head over his arm for a closer inspection of the wound. "It looks like it's full of dirt and hair."

Above her head, Adam smiled. After a week of cool indifference, her show of concern was like a soothing balm. "Horsehair and a little dirt aren't going to kill me."

"No. But the bacteria will deal that arm some misery if you don't let me clean it out. Where's a first-aid kit?"

He could just hear the wranglers and Anna laughing about his needing first aid for a rope burn. "I'll deal with it later."

"I know how you'll deal with it," she said, leaning back and glancing up at his face. "You'll turn the tap water on it for a few seconds and say that's clean enough."

He grinned, and Maureen wondered why he had to be so damn charming even when he wasn't trying.

"It's always worked before," he said.

"Well, not this time. So where's the antiseptic?"

"Okay, I give up. I'll go after the first-aid kit. But no bandages," he forewarned. "I'm not ready to be the laughingstock of the ranch."

Maureen was waiting for him at the kitchen table when he returned with a small plastic case of medical supplies. She immediately straightened his arm out on the tabletop and clucked her tongue at the damage.

"This is really awful," she murmured as she

poured a generous portion of peroxide over the wound, then went to work with a cotton swab. "How did you do it anyway?"

"Trying to hold eight hundred pounds of nervous horseflesh while my sister used electric clippers on his mane."

"Then your sister knows you were hurt?"

"Oh, yeah," he said with a shrug. Then deciding it wouldn't hurt to garner all the sympathy he could get, he added, "She said she was sorry, then laughed."

"Laughed! But that's horrible!"

Adam had to chuckle. "Not really. Anna knows her brother is tough. Besides, it's just a bad rope burn. Every cowboy gets them from time to time."

Her gaze lifted to his face. "You consider yourself a cowboy?"

"I was a cowboy long before I ever got into the gas business," he said easily.

"You like the profession," she stated rather than questioned.

"Always have. But I like drilling for petroleum, too. The payoff is almost always better."

She continued to swab the wound. "I didn't realize money was your main objective."

"It isn't. But it's a nice dividend, don't you think?"

Maureen thought she'd trade all the money she had in the world to have a home and family as Adam had, but he obviously wouldn't understand that. He'd never been entirely alone. He didn't know what it did to a person's heart.

"You know, Maureen," he said after a few moments passed, "I'm glad…you're talking to me again."

She glanced up from his arm, then wished she hadn't. His face was so close. Too close for her rattled senses. "I never quit."

His gaze dropped to her berry-red lips. "You've been avoiding me like the plague," he accused.

"I could say the same about you." Shaken by the touch of his eyes, she turned her attention back to his arm. "Besides, Adam, we agreed we weren't…well, that we need to keep things cool between us."

He sighed. "Yes, I know we agreed. But that doesn't mean we have to treat each other quite so coldly. I don't like working that way. I don't like…being that way with you."

Her hand stilled on his arm, and for a moment she allowed herself to savor the feel of his warm skin, the fine hair curling around her fingers. All week she'd yearned to touch him. She supposed the injury had been a good excuse.

"I'm not crazy about it, either," she admitted lowly.

"Then do you think we can be friends again?"

A voice of warning shouted in her head, but she could hardly hear it over the drumming of her heart.

"I don't believe…"

When she didn't go on, Adam took hold of her chin and lifted her face up to his. "Believe what?" he prompted.

She swallowed as her senses scattered like dry leaves in a fall wind. "That we can…ever be friends. There's too much—"

"Chemistry between us," he finished wryly.

At least he hadn't called it lust, Maureen thought

gratefully. Nodding, she said, "Something like that. And if we try to be friends—"

"We *are* friends," he interrupted. "You just don't want to admit it."

Maybe he was right. They weren't strangers. Nor were they simply co-workers. Friends would be the safest label to put on their relationship.

"All right," she agreed. "We're friends."

"Good," he said, flashing her another grin. "I think we should start all over again."

"And how do you propose we do that? We've already started over once since I broke your ankle."

He shook his head. "Forget about my ankle. Forget our swim. Forget about this damn burn on my arm. Let's go down to the barn and find a couple of riding horses. You can ride a horse, can't you?"

"If it's docile enough."

"I can probably find a nag among the bunch."

She smoothed antibiotic cream over the long patch of raw flesh, then covered the whole thing with three Band-Aid strips.

"And where am I going to ride this nag?" she wanted to know.

"Just out on the mesa. Or we can ride south to the mountains. I'd like to show you some of the ranch. So far, you've only seen the house and the ranch yard."

To get outdoors and enjoy the balmy summer evening would be nice, Maureen thought. And if being alone with Adam was the equivalent of trying to diet in a candy store, then she could view it as a test or preparation of sorts. Because sooner or later, their job would send them off together and she was going to have to be prepared.

"Okay," she said with a shrug, "I accept your invitation. Just don't expect me to ride like a cowgirl."

The corner of his mouth lifted, exposing his straight white teeth. "I don't expect you to be anything but yourself."

Chapter Five

The so-called nag Adam picked out for Maureen turned out to be a piebald gray who'd been ridden the day before gathering cattle in the mountains. The work had knocked the "edge" off him, Adam assured her, so he wouldn't feel like kicking up his heels.

"But I don't want to ride a tired horse!" Maureen exclaimed. "That's cruel."

Adam laughed as he tugged the saddle cinch tight against the animal's underbelly. "Leo is anything but tired. He's just burned enough energy yesterday to make him manageable today." He turned and motioned his head toward the seat of the saddle. "He's ready. Want me to help you mount?"

"I think I can manage on my own." She stepped up carefully to the horse and lifted her toe toward the dangling stirrup. "Wasn't Leo a foot shorter a moment ago?"

"Don't insult his Thoroughbred blood," Adam said with a chuckle, then not bothering to ask permission, he planted his palm against Maureen's rear and shoved.

She squealed loudly and grabbed the saddle horn as the strength of his unexpected boost sent her very nearly over the horse's back.

"You just had to do that, didn't you? What would you have done if I'd fallen off on the other side?" she demanded.

Her breasts were heaving and part of her disheveled hair clung to the side of her face. She looked so gorgeous he had half a mind to drag her out of the saddle and do it all over again. "Picked you up, dusted you off and put you back on Leo."

Maureen rolled her eyes. "Is this the way you treat all your female friends?" she asked, then shook her head. "Don't answer. I remember now. You don't invite your women friends out here. Only your female enemies."

Laughing heartily, he untethered the chestnut waiting a few steps away and swung easily into the saddle. "I didn't know a scientist could possess a bit of wit, too. You must be a rare breed."

No. She wasn't rare, Maureen thought. More like crazy for ever agreeing to go with Adam on this excursion. And perhaps even crazier for coming to New Mexico in the first place.

Yet in spite of her doubts and worries about Adam, something kept on telling her this place was meant to be her home. And she prayed her instincts weren't leading her to a broken heart.

Wranglers were busy with the evening chores as Maureen and Adam rode through the dusty ranch yard. Several of the men lifted hands in greeting and called to Adam. When they rode past the long white building of horse stables, Anna was outside, hosing down a painted colt. She waved to the two of them, and Maureen waved back.

"Seeing your sister like this, it's hard to believe she used to be a concert pianist," Maureen told him.

Adam had chosen to ride along a cattle trail headed south of the ranch and into the mountains. So far, the open ground allowed them to ride abreast, and now that Maureen had spoken, he glanced across at her. "I'll have her play for you sometime. She can work magic with a piano."

Maureen had first met Adam's twin a couple of days ago at the ranch house and she'd liked the other woman immediately. She was as beautiful and vibrant as her mother. And she seemed extraordinarily close to her brother.

"I can't imagine her giving it up. Some people study all their lives just to get the opportunity to do what she was doing."

Adam nodded. "That's true. But she hasn't really given up her music. Now she can play when she wants to and for whom she wants to. And believe me, my sister is much happier now that she's left that life behind and married Miguel."

"Has she always been interested in horses?"

Adam laughed. "*Obsessed* is more the word. She's just like Mom. It's something that's in her blood and she's damn good at it. I think that's one reason why she was never truly happy while she was touring with her music career. She missed the ranch and the horses and the simpleness of it all."

Maureen had often wondered what her life might be like if she didn't work as a geologist. Would she be happier if she simplified her life with a regular nine-to-five job? She somehow doubted it. No one was at home waiting for her, wanting her. And as for anyone needing her, she supposed no one ever had. Except her daughter. And when the baby had needed her the most, she'd failed her. But she didn't want to think of that now. She tried not ever to think of it.

"Your sister is a lucky woman," Maureen said. "But even more brave, I think."

"Why so?" Adam asked curiously.

"Because she followed her heart instead of trudging along the expected course."

He smiled faintly. "And you think that takes a lot of courage?"

"I'm sure of it."

The warm rays of the sinking sun caught in her long hair and bathed her skin with a golden glow. As Adam's gaze lingered on the soft profile of her features, then dipped to the generous thrust of her breasts he knew he'd never seen a more sensual woman. She'd been made to love a man and have his children. So why was she alone? he wondered. And why could he not bear to picture any man touching her except himself?

For the next few minutes they rode in silence. Little by little, the trail narrowed and began to climb through a stand of ponderosa pine.

When it finally became impossible to ride side by side, Maureen was content to let Adam take the lead and allow Leo to follow at a slower pace. Eventually, the forest thickened. Spruce and aspen became interspersed among the tall pines. Chipmunks scurried across the forest floor and more than once deer bolted from the shadows, then bounded gracefully out of sight.

Maureen drank in the quiet beauty of it all and thought how wonderful it was that the Sanderses owned land that would be handed down through generations and never be marred by the progress of civilization.

When the rocky path they were traveling finally became almost too steep to go on, it curved around the side of the mountain and Maureen gasped at the sudden splendor spreading out below her.

A few feet ahead, a break in the cliff widened the trail. Adam pulled his chestnut to a halt and Maureen stopped Leo directly behind him. He twisted in his saddle and smiled back at her. "Beautiful, isn't it?"

"Breathtaking," she agreed.

"Would you like to get off and stretch your legs?"

By now, stiffness was creeping into Maureen's bottom half. She wasn't sure she'd be able to get off Leo, much less get back on him.

"I don't know if that would be a very good idea," she said as she tried to draw her feet out of the stirrups. "I thought I was in fair shape until I got on this horse."

"Riding takes muscles you didn't know you had," he told her. "Just wait a minute, and I'll help you down."

She remained where she was while he dismounted and tethered the chestnut to a nearby juniper bush. When he returned to her and Leo, she didn't have much choice but to lift her right leg over the saddle horn and slide into his outstretched arms.

Maureen anchored her hands on his shoulders and he gripped her rib cage as he took the brunt of her weight, then set her gently down on the ground.

"How's the legs?" he asked, his hands lingering on the curve of her waist.

"Like two pieces of rubber," she admitted with a shaky laugh. "But I'll manage."

Once Adam was sure she could stand on her own, he took Leo by the reins and tethered him to the trunk of a spindly piñon pine, then came back to her. "Come on," he said, "let's walk over to the edge of the cliff and take a look. The exercise will help you get your feet back under you."

She nodded, and with his hand plastered to the small of her back, they slowly made their way over the rocky, uneven ground. If he was using the wobbly condition of her legs for a reason to touch her, Maureen certainly wasn't going to make an issue of it. This evening spent with him had been too nice to spoil it for any reason. And she couldn't deny, even to herself, how good the support of his hand felt against her.

Several feet from the edge of the cliff, Adam warned, "This is far enough. The soil is loamy and crumbles easily. If we toppled over the side of the mountain, it would be days before anyone found us. And by then, the coyotes and buzzards would have picked our bones clean."

She cast him a sardonic glance. "Now you've ruined the beauty of the place."

Chuckling, he motioned for her to look at the view rather than at him. "You can almost see all the way to Alamogordo from here."

"I didn't realize the desert was so near," she said. "I thought more mountains would be behind this one."

"You might call that land down there desert. But I call it good grazing."

Her expression turned thoughtful. "You know, I believe you're just as much a rancher as you are an oilman."

Adam glanced down at her with mild surprise. "I never thought about it much. But you might be right. I wouldn't like my life without land or cows or horses in it."

She smiled faintly. "Then you're as unique as a scientist with wit. Because all the men I've ever worked with in the oil and gas business are definitely one-dimensional. Their whole world revolves around getting gas or oil from the ground as fast as they can."

"Hmm. I have to admit you're right. Most of them don't have outside interests. As for me, I like the business and I want to do well in it. But I guess I have too much of my father in me to be just an oilman."

She glanced curiously up at him. "What do you mean? Your father is an oilman."

Smiling, he shook his head, then with a nudge against her back, guided her over to a flat boulder. Maureen took a seat on one end and waited for him to join her.

After he'd stretched his long legs out in front of him and lifted his hat to run a hand over his hair, he said, "I guess this will probably surprise you, though it's not really a secret. Wyatt is not my real father."

Maureen's brows shot up, but Adam tugged the brim of his hat back down on his forehead before she could say anything.

"What I mean," Adam went on, "is that he's not

the man who sired me. Wyatt is actually my uncle and Chloe my half sister.''

She let out a soft gasp. "Your half sister? And uncle? I don't understand!''

He shrugged. "I didn't expect you to. It's all rather complicated.''

Maureen gently placed her hand on his thigh. "If you'd rather not tell me, I'll understand.''

He gave her a sidelong glance and could see in her eyes that she did understand and wouldn't think less of him if he changed the subject completely. Just knowing she felt that way drew him to her in a way he'd never expected.

"It's all right. I don't mind talking about it. I'm certainly not ashamed of my heritage. In fact, my birth father is somewhat of a legend in this area. He bought this land more than sixty years ago and built the Bar M virtually by himself. From what my mom and aunts, or maybe I should say my half sisters tell me, Tomas Murdock was a hardworking, boisterous man who liked to drink and gamble. He loved horses even more. On or off the racetrack. When his wife's health failed, he became involved with another woman, Wyatt's sister, Belinda. The two of them had a secret affair and as a result Anna and I were born.''

"So what happened to your birth parents?'' Maureen had to ask. "Where are they now?''

His features were suddenly clouded with regret. "I'm sorry to say they're both dead. Shortly after Anna and I were born, Tomas suffered a fatal heart attack. He was only in his mid-fifties, but from what I've been told, they'd been hard-lived years.''

Fascinated, Maureen urged him to go on. "And

Belinda? She must have been much younger if she was able to bear children."

Adam nodded. "Close to twenty-five years younger. But she had emotional problems, and they were compounded when she believed Tomas had deserted her and the two babies."

"Had he deserted her and you children?" Maureen asked, surprised at how much she truly wanted to know about this man.

"We don't believe so. My sisters discovered many canceled checks he'd been sending to Belinda. She was living in Las Cruces at the time, and we suppose when the checks and Tomas quit coming to her, she snapped. She left Anna and me in a laundry basket on the front porch of the ranch house."

Maureen's head swung slowly from side to side as she tried to digest all that he'd told her. It was all so difficult to imagine that this strong, confident, sexy man beside her had come into the world under such circumstances. She'd figured his life had been charmed from the moment he'd drawn his first breath.

"Oh, my, Adam. I can't...I just find this so hard to believe."

"Well, believe it. She did. Justine found us, and for a good while, none of them even knew we were Murdocks, too."

Incredulous, Maureen stared at him. "You mean Belinda disappeared? She didn't let anyone know she'd left you behind?"

He shook his head. "No. It's a long story, but eventually she was found and placed in a mental facility. She died there shortly afterward."

"So Chloe and Wyatt stepped in as your parents," she said, stating the obvious.

"Because of us twins, they met and fell in love. After they married, they adopted us as their own children. But they never tried to keep our true heritage a secret. In fact, Dad has a diary of Belinda's, which was written during the time she was having the affair with Tomas. Perhaps you'd like to read it sometime. The entries aren't always happy. But it's interesting. She was an intelligent woman. Until the love affair broke her heart and sapped her spirit. But that oftentimes happens when one person cares too much for another."

Maureen wondered if he was speaking from personal experience. And she wanted to ask him if he'd ever cared about a woman too much for his own good, but she couldn't bring herself to utter the question. Somehow she didn't want to think he'd ever truly given his heart to any female.

"So you think that's what happened to your mother? She cared too much for your father?"

He didn't answer immediately, and she studied his profile as he gazed out at the endless plain stretching below them. He was not the man she'd first thought him to be. He was more. Much more.

The faint smile on his face as he turned to look at her was both wry and sad. "I'm certain of it."

So that was how Adam thought of love, Maureen concluded. He believed it was something that ruined people, that it had killed his mother and perhaps even his father.

For years now, Maureen had held the same notion. Caring about someone too much could only lead to destruction. She'd chiseled the wisdom into the stone that used to be her heart, and for all this time, even in her loneliest of moments, she'd not forgotten it.

Here's a 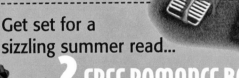 HOT offer for you!

Get set for a sizzling summer read...

with **2 FREE ROMANCE BOOKS** and a **FREE MYSTERY GIFT!**

NO CATCH! NO OBLIGATION TO BUY!

Simply complete and return this card and you'll get **FREE BOOKS, A FREE GIFT** and much more!

- 🌀 The first shipment is yours to keep, **absolutely free!**

- 🌀 Enjoy the convenience of romance books, delivered right to your door, before they're available in the stores!

- 🌀 Take advantage of special low pricing for **Reader Service Members only!**

- 🌀 After receiving your free books we hope you'll want to remain a subscriber. But the choice is always yours—to continue or cancel anytime at all! So why not take us up on this fabulous invitation with no risk of any kind. You'll be glad you did!

315 SDL CPSQ

215 SDL CPSH
S-R-05/99

▼ DETACH HERE AND MAIL CARD TODAY! ▼

Name:	
	(Please Print)
Address:	Apt.#:
City:	
State/Prov.:	Zip/ Postal Code:

The Silhouette Reader Service™ —Here's How it Works:

Accepting your 2 free books and mystery gift places you under no obligation to buy anything. You may keep the books and gift and return the shipping statement marked "cancel." If you do not cancel, about a month later we'll send you 6 additional novels and bill you just $2.90 each in the U.S., or $3.25 each in Canada, plus 25¢ delivery per book and applicable taxes if any.* That's the complete price and — compared to the cover price of $3.50 in the U.S. and $3.99 in Canada — it's quite a bargain! You may cancel at any time, but if you choose to continue, every month we'll send you 6 more books, which you may either purchase at the discount price or return to us and cancel your subscription.

*Terms and prices subject to change without notice. Sales tax applicable in N.Y. Canadian residents will be charged applicable provincial taxes and GST.

If offer card is missing write to: Silhouette Reader Service, 3010 Walden Ave., P.O. Box 1867, Buffalo, NY 14240-1867

BUSINESS REPLY MAIL
FIRST-CLASS MAIL   PERMIT NO. 717   BUFFALO, NY

POSTAGE WILL BE PAID BY ADDRESSEE

SILHOUETTE READER SERVICE
3010 WALDEN AVE
PO BOX 1867
BUFFALO NY 14240-9952

NO POSTAGE
NECESSARY
IF MAILED
IN THE
UNITED STATES

But now as she looked at him, she thought how sad it was that he didn't want to give his heart. Maureen had a right to feel jaded and ruined. Adam didn't. Or did he? she wondered.

"Is that why you've never married? Because of what happened all those years ago to your birth parents?" she asked before she could stop herself.

The moment the question was out, she could see a door slam shut inside his dark green eyes.

"Why I've never married is none of your business."

His words stung even though she told herself they shouldn't. "I told you about my divorce," she reminded him.

"Look, Maureen, I have my own private demons just like you. And they're not something I want to share with anyone."

Not even with her. He'd made that perfectly clear, and she had to let it go at that, Maureen told herself. She was supposed to be his friend, nothing more. And as his friend, she had to respect his privacy.

"Sure. I understand," she murmured, then forced herself to smile up at him.

Something flickered in his eyes and he looked away from her and out toward the distant horizon. "The sun has already set," he said gruffly. "We'd better start back to the ranch before it gets too dark."

He rose to his feet and reached his hand down for her. She took it, then he tugged her gently up beside him. Tilting her head back, she looked up at him, and for a moment the longing to kiss him was so strong she could scarcely breathe.

"Thank you, Adam."

His eyelids lowered as his gaze lingered on the moist curve of her lips. "For what?"

She swallowed and swiftly glanced down at the toes of his boots. "For this ride. And for telling me the story about your parents."

He grimaced. "I don't know why I did. I'm sure you found it boring."

She forced herself to laugh, then pulling her hand free of his, she started back to the horses. "I'm the one who's as boring as vanilla pudding," she called over her shoulder.

Adam could have told her his favorite flavor was vanilla. He could have gone after her and took pleasure in tasting the sweetness of her lips. But he'd made a pact with her to be *just friends*. And he couldn't risk jeopardizing the fragile truce they'd struck between them. This past week, he'd learned that having her company like this was much better than not having her company at all.

The next morning, Maureen was surprised when Adam invited her to ride into work with him rather than drive her own vehicle.

A week ago, she would have instantly found an excuse not to accept his offer of a lift. But after last night, she was beginning to believe he really did want their relationship to be friendly. And since they were both going and returning to the same place, Maureen decided taking one vehicle would be the practical thing to do.

The twenty-mile trip into town passed quickly as they discussed the day's schedule ahead of them. Once there, Adam stopped at a bakery long enough to let Maureen pick up a couple of sweet rolls, then she went to work in the lab and he in his office. She didn't see him again until quitting time that evening when he came back to the lab to fetch her.

"Ready to go home?" he called to her.

Maureen looked up from the microscope and glanced over her shoulder to see him standing in the doorway. He was dressed more like a businessman today, in dark trousers and a white shirt. The clothes gave him a suave appearance that no doubt turned the heads of all the secretaries and VIPs who met with him. But as for Maureen, she preferred to think of him as he'd been last night—in old boots and jeans, the battered gray hat dipped low on his forehead and a shadow of beard on his face.

Slipping off her glasses, she said, "Just give me a minute to put these tests away."

"I'm in no hurry," he said, then walked over to where she was stashing away several tubes of soil and sludge. "In fact, I hope you're not in a big rush to get home. I'd like to drop by my place to see how the carpenters are faring."

She hadn't expected him to be making a detour this evening. But after last night she could hardly suspect his motives. If he'd really wanted to try to take up where they left off at the swimming pool, he'd had plenty of opportunities. In fact, the more Maureen thought about it, the more confused she became.

From the moment she arrived to work at Sanders, she'd told herself she couldn't let anything happen between her and Adam. She'd promised herself she wouldn't allow anything to happen. But still, she had to admit it had been deflating, even disappointing, last night when he hadn't kissed her. And the whole situation was making her wonder if she was losing her mind.

"That's fine with me," she told him. "I don't have any errands to run."

Adam helped her put away the last of the material she'd been using, then the two of them left the building through a back exit. Outside, the evening sun was still hot and it burned through Maureen's thin blouse as they walked to Adam's truck.

"I still haven't gotten used to the climate here," she admitted to him. "During the day I nearly keel over from the heat and at night I'm shivering. Does it never change?"

"In the winter. It stays cold all the time. After the years you've spent living in Houston, all the snow might have you deciding you don't want to live here after all."

Was that what he was hoping for? she wondered, then shook away the suspicious thought. It didn't matter whether Adam wanted her here or not. She'd come to Ruidoso and Sanders to make a new life for herself. Adam Murdock Sanders wasn't going to be a part of it.

"I'm not about to let a little snow run me off," she assured him. "I'm not that soft."

Adam's gaze drifted over the length of her. Normally, she wore jeans and hiking boots to work, but today she was dressed in fluttery, wide-legged slacks and a sleeveless blouse that was so sheer he could see the faint outline of lacy lingerie beneath it. The image had haunted him all day. And he wondered how he could keep on pretending he didn't want her.

The trip to Adam's place took thirty minutes over a mountainous dirt road. Maureen hadn't expected him to live in such a secluded place and was even more surprised when they drove up to a modest ranch-style house built of chinked logs. Knowing his wealth, she'd expected him to live in something a little showier.

"It's beautiful," she said as they stepped down from the pickup truck.

His glance at her was full of doubt. "You really think so?"

"Of course," she said with a puzzled smile. "Don't you?"

He shrugged, then motioned for her to follow him to the front door. "I suppose. When I first bought the place several years ago, I had high hopes for it. But now...well, I guess it still needs a little more work."

They stepped through the front door and into a small foyer. Immediately, the smell of sawdust and paint stripper filled her nostrils, and from somewhere in the back of the house a power saw buzzed loudly.

In the living room, Adam guided her around a stack of drywall and several buckets of paint, then down a long hallway. As Maureen followed him, she could see the house was very roomy and had obviously been in excellent condition before the carpenters had started their work.

Two men were busy in the kitchen. One was at work removing varnish from knotty-pine cabinets Maureen would have loved to have in her own house.

As soon as the carpenters spotted the visitors, they descended on Adam and immediately began to discuss the progress of the renovations. Maureen made herself scarce and wandered back through the other parts of the house.

She looked over every room, then returned to the

living area and lingered there for several minutes while Adam continued his discussion with the carpenters. Eventually, she gave up on him and slipped out a sliding glass door and onto a low patio built of redwood planks.

Unlike the place Maureen had bought, Adam's house sat in a clearing at the base of a mountain. The land was more open and arid here. Rather than spruce and tall pine, the trees were mostly piñon, scrubby cottonwood and poplar. Clumps of yucca and cholla grew with wild abandon right up to the patio floor.

She took a seat at a wooden picnic table shaded by a cottonwood. A barbecue pit built of red brick stood a few feet away, and she wondered how often Adam entertained guests here. Or more important, if a woman had ever lived here with him. In spite of its beauty, there was a lonely, primitive feel about the place. She couldn't picture him living in this isolated spot alone and liking it. But then she didn't really know the man. Not the way she wanted to know him.

"There you are."

She glanced around to see him stepping out the glass door and onto the patio. "I decided to look around outside," she told him. "It's very pretty. I get the feeling I'm sitting right in the middle of the desert."

He groaned inwardly at the charming picture she made there in the dappled shade with the south wind whipping her loose brown hair and molding her clothes against the curves of her body. Since the night in the pool, he hadn't kissed her, but the memory was constantly urging him to. And he wasn't sure how much longer he could fight it.

Trying to shake away the thought, he walked over

to where she sat. "People who aren't from these parts are amazed at how quickly the landscape around here changes from forested mountains to desert."

Expecting he was ready to go, Maureen rose to her feet. "Speaking of changes," she said, "I don't understand what you're doing to your house."

His brows lifted. "What do you mean? I'm renovating it."

She frowned at him. "I understand that much. But why? From what I can see, the inside of the house was beautiful before you ever started. And those kitchen cabinets—you're going to ruin them if you don't leave them as they are."

He jammed his hands into his trouser pockets. Mostly to keep from touching her. "That's your opinion."

Her lips pressed together at his curt response. "Well, I know you didn't ask for it. I just can't figure out what you're trying to do with the place."

He looked away from her and thoughtfully back at the house. "I've lived here for six years and I like the place. But when I walk through the front door, it still doesn't quite have that feeling of home to it. Do you know what I mean?"

Maureen knew all too well what he meant. She'd been searching for the same place, but in the back of her mind, she was wise enough to know she would more than likely never find it. When her baby daughter had died, her home had died with her.

"Adam, I think..." She stopped with a shake of her head.

A frown marred his face as he glanced back at her. "Go on," he urged. "I told you last night I'd rather you speak your mind with me."

"I'm not so sure you knew what you'd be getting into when you said that. But all right. I think you need to understand that rooms or the shape and color of them do not make a home."

He cocked an arrogant brow at her. "Is that so?"

She nodded.

He slowly folded his arms across his chest. "Well, in my opinion, if a house *looks* like a home, it will *feel* like one."

Her short laugh mocked his words. "And how do you make a house look like a home?"

With a grimace, he turned and walked over to the edge of the patio and gazed at the western horizon. The sun was sinking behind a ridge of low, rolling mountains and the heat of the day was following it. Adam wished his thoughts of Maureen would also cool with the setting sun.

"You really don't want to hear this," he said.

She went over to him and he gave her a sidelong glance. "Yes, I do want to hear it," she told him. "I'm very interested to hear about these marvelous decorating skills. I might want to use them on my new house after I move in."

That she was mocking him was obvious to Adam, but he wasn't exactly sure why. Where Maureen was concerned he wasn't sure about anything. Except that he wanted her with an appetite that was far from healthy.

"What is this, anyway?" he asked with an annoyed frown. "If you think I'm wrecking the house, just tell me."

She sighed. He was getting defensive and she shouldn't have said anything. After all, what he did with this place was none of her business. "I don't necessarily think you're ruining your house. I just believe you're deluding yourself.''

"Oh, so now I'm delusional,'' he muttered, his green eyes rolling toward the sky. "When I tell you to speak your mind, you don't hold anything back, do you?''

"Not much,'' she agreed.

"Okay. Since you seem to be so smug and all-knowing about this, why don't you give me a hint and tell me what you think my house needs. Selling?''

She frowned at him and shook her head. "No. It's a perfectly lovely place. Or it would be if you'd have those carpenters put it back together and get the heck out of there. Because the only way you can make your house look like a home is to fill it with a wife and children.''

Adam looked at her as if she'd just instructed him to shoot himself. "You're kidding, aren't you?''

She shook her head again. "I'm very serious. You could knock out walls, build more cabinets, change the wallpaper, but none of those things would make any difference. They're not going to make it feel any more like home to you than it does now.''

His eyes narrowed and his jaw turned to rock. After a moment, he said, "You have some nerve telling me this, Maureen. You're divorced and from what you've told me you don't want to be married.''

"That's true,'' she conceded. "But that's all about me. Not about you.''

He snorted. "Well, there's no way in hell I'm going to marry and have kids. No way!''

The fierceness in his voice took Maureen aback. It was one thing to believe marriage wasn't his cup of tea, but he was roaring like an angry lion.

"Why?" she dared to ask.

His features turned even harder. "I told you last night, Maureen. Why I haven't married is none of your business! I don't know why you keep bringing it up!"

Maureen didn't know, either. Nor did she understand why it hurt to have him shut her out this way. But it did. The sting of rejection burned through her body.

"I had the stupid notion you might—" She broke off abruptly and turned away from him.

"Go ahead and finish!" he barked. "Hellfire, you've already said plenty. You might as well add a little more to your sage advice."

She stared at him for several long, pointed moments. Then finally she said, "If you're quite finished making an ass of yourself, I'm ready to go."

Something about the quietness of her voice brought him up short, and as the anger clouding his vision cleared, he could see Maureen's expression was completely closed off to him.

Heaving out a breath, Adam turned his back to her and raked a hand through his hair. He hadn't meant to hurt her. He didn't even know why he'd let her suggestion get to him. Plenty of friends and family had told him he needed to get married. He'd let their remarks roll off his back like water on a duck's feathers.

But hell, he silently cursed, Maureen shouldn't have been digging. She didn't need to know he'd once wanted a wife and children or that he'd planned to have one of those *real* homes she'd been talking about. She didn't need to know all his hopes and dreams had died along with his fiancée. He didn't share that pain in his heart with anyone. Not even his family.

"Maureen, I..." Rubbing a hand over his eyes, he turned back around only to find he was standing alone and Maureen was nowhere in sight.

He found her waiting in the pickup. She said nothing when he slid behind the wheel and started the engine, but as he headed down the dusty road away from the house, she turned her head and looked at him.

"By the way, I didn't divorce my husband. He left me."

Adam glanced over at her wounded face and knew there was nothing he could say now. He'd already said too much.

Chapter Six

"I told the tool pusher you'd be out at the rig Wednesday morning. By nine at the least. That won't be a problem, will it?"

While his father spoke, Adam's gaze remained on the picture window to the left of his desk. The sky had grown dark in the past hour and now lightning sizzled over the distant mountains. But his mind wasn't on the weather. It really wasn't on anything except Maureen.

"No problem."

"Good. Because you're to meet with the mud people in Bloomfield for lunch. And when you do, I want you to be sure and get it across to them that we don't intend to be robbed. We'll call a company out of Farmington if we have to."

"Fine."

Wyatt walked over to the window and deliberately put himself in front of Adam's vacant stare. "Are you with me on this, Adam, or should I make the trip myself?''

Adam drew a hand over his face and jerked his feet down from the corner of the desk. ''Of course I'm with you,'' he said gruffly. ''I'll be there. And I'll deal with the mud company.''

Wyatt studied his son for long, silent moments. ''Are you all right?''

Adam's gaze flew to his father. ''Why, yes,'' he snapped. ''Why shouldn't I be?''

Wyatt shook his head. ''I don't know. Why shouldn't you? It's not like you've been swamped with work the past couple of days. You've had a little leisure time. And you said the carpenters were making headway with your house.''

Since his and Maureen's visit to the house two days ago, he'd told the carpenters to put everything back as best they could and be on their way. Fortunately, he'd been paying them by the hour so there'd been no dispute about a written contract.

''Yeah. They should have things finished in a couple of weeks,'' he said.

''Two weeks! Those men couldn't possibly do what you've planned in that length of time.''

Adam shook his head and rose to his feet. ''I've decided to scrap most of the changes.''

Wyatt's brows lifted skeptically. ''Really? What brought this about?''

Adam shrugged and headed for the coffeepot. The glass carafe held an inch of tarry black liquid. Deciding he didn't want anything to drink after all, he shoved the pot back onto the warmer.

''Oh, I got to thinking the house is fine like it is.

Besides, it's time I got back home and out of your and Mom's hair.''

Wyatt dismissed his excuse with a short laugh. ''We rarely see you at the Bar M. You couldn't be bothering us. But if Maureen's presence there is annoying you, then you might be glad to know she's going to be moving into her own house in the next day or two.''

Adam's head jerked around toward his father. ''Moving! Who said?''

''She did. She hasn't mentioned it to you?''

Since their stopover at Adam's the other evening, Maureen hadn't mentioned much at all to him. The past two days he'd invited her to ride into work with him, but both times she'd refused with the excuse that she had errands to run in town. He'd put a wall between them that he didn't know how to break down and he was beginning to wonder if Maureen had been right after all when she'd said they could never be friends.

''No. She hasn't mentioned it,'' he said with as much indifference as he could manage. ''But it doesn't matter to me one way or the other when she moves.'' Wyatt suddenly chuckled and the sound grated on Adam's raw nerves. ''Something funny about that?''

''No. I'm just laughing because you're such a terrible liar.''

Adam's expression turned wary. It wasn't like his dad to tease him about a woman. In fact, Wyatt rarely made mention of any of the women he'd dated in the past. Why should he have the notion Maureen might be special?

"Maureen is no different to me than the secretary sitting in the next room," Adam assured him.

Wyatt let out another chuckle, which annoyed Adam even more. "Then I guess it wouldn't bother you any if she started seeing someone on a regular basis?"

Regular basis! Hell, it would bother him on a one-time basis, Adam thought. But she wouldn't date, he silently argued with himself. She didn't want anything to do with a man.

Unless the right one came along, a little voice inside him mocked.

"Maureen isn't seeing anyone," Adam said sharply.

"No. But your mother and I were thinking we should introduce her to some of the eligible men around here. The woman is bound to be lonely."

"Lonely! Hell, she has plenty of work to do."

Wyatt moved from his spot by the window and headed toward the door. "Chloe and I have plenty of work to keep us busy, too. But we still need each other. And I don't mean just to talk, either."

Adam had never heard his father talk exactly this way before and he could only stare at him with raised eyebrows. "Don't you think Maureen would rather do her own choosing?" he asked the older man.

"Of course," Wyatt answered. "Your mother just wants to give her something to choose from."

As far as Adam was concerned, his mother needed to quit her infernal matchmaking. And he was about to tell his father that exact thing when the telephone on his desk rang and thankfully put an end to their conversation.

* * *

Later that evening when Maureen entered the back gate of the Bar M courtyard, she stepped into what appeared to be some sort of family party. Feeling immediately like an intruder, she stood just inside the gate, trying to decide whether to turn around and head back to her pickup truck or make a dash for the house.

She decided on the latter and was slipping along the edge of the porch, trying not to draw attention to herself, when Chloe came up behind her and grabbed her by the elbow.

"Maureen, I didn't see you arrive! Don't run off. Everyone is starting to eat." She began to tug Maureen from the porch and toward a group of people crowded around a long table.

Maureen quickly began to protest. "Chloe, I'm not really dressed for a party. And I can see this is a family affair."

"Nonsense. None of us is dressed up. Your jeans are fine. And you're certainly welcome to join our family gathering. We're just having a little birthday supper for Miguel."

Maureen glanced around her. From an earlier meeting, she recognized Chloe's sisters, Justine and Rose. She'd also met Anna's husband, Miguel, who was apparently the guest of honor tonight. The remainder of the group she didn't know. Except for Adam, and he wasn't anywhere in sight. Yet she knew he had to be here somewhere. She'd just parked by his pickup.

"I'm really not all that hungry, Chloe. But if you insist, I'll eat."

"Of course I insist. Just jump in and make a hog of yourself." She patted Maureen's arm. "Now if you'll excuse me, I've got to go check on the dessert."

What Chloe called a little supper was a feast, even in Texas terms. Containers of barbecued ribs, fried chicken, potato salad and coleslaw were heaped from one end of the table to the other.

Someone pushed a paper plate into her hand and made a place for her in the serving line. Maureen filled the plate and carried it and a paper cup of iced tea over to an inconspicuous spot on the ground-level porch.

She'd taken three bites when a blond woman carrying a plate laden with food approached her. As she drew closer, Maureen noticed she appeared to be in her second trimester of pregnancy.

"Hi," she said warmly. "I'm Emily Dunn. Adam and Anna's cousin."

Maureen smiled at the other woman. "Hello. I'm Maureen. Or did you know that already?"

Emily smiled and nodded as she eased herself down into a lawn chair facing Maureen. "Chloe's told us about you."

"About her pestering houseguest, I'm sure."

"Not at all. She's sorry you'll soon be moving out. Chloe loves people. Almost as much as her horses."

As Emily talked and the two of them began to eat, Maureen's eyes drifted to the woman's stomach. "Is this your first child you're expecting?" Maureen asked more out of politeness than anything else. Pregnant women bothered her. She didn't want to be reminded of the joy she felt when she'd carried her own daughter inside her womb. Or the terrible grief when she'd lost her.

"No. I have a two-year-old son, Harlan Cooper. He's back there somewhere with his daddy." She smiled at Maureen. "Chloe says you're from Houston. How do you like it here in New Mexico?"

"The climate is more extreme than I imagined. But I like it very much."

"I'm glad. Maybe one of our good men around here will catch your eye and then you'll be well and truly rooted to the area."

"There aren't any good men around here."

Both women turned their heads to see Adam striding up with a little blond boy riding on his shoulders and obviously loving every minute of it.

"Adam!" Emily scolded. "You know that's not true. You're here, aren't you?"

A wry grin twisted his lips. "Am I supposed to be good?"

Emily chuckled. "Well, that's stretching the imagination a bit. Half the female population of this county would testify you're a devil."

Adam glanced at Maureen. Pink color bathed the ridge of her cheekbones and her lips were compressed in a thin line. She obviously wasn't happy to see him, and the idea bothered him far more than he wanted to admit.

"Mommy, I'm hungry," the youngster on Adam's shoulders suddenly wailed.

"Well, you can't eat up there," Emily told her son. "Unless you use the top of Adam's head for a table."

"I'm not ready for that," Adam said with a laugh, then carefully set the boy down on the porch. "I'll take him to a real table and fix him a plate," he told Emily.

"I'll do it," Emily said, already rising to her feet. "I want to make sure he eats more than just birthday cake." She glanced over at Maureen. "Nice meeting you. Maybe we can talk more before the evening is over."

"Yes, I'd like that," Maureen said.

The woman led the child away and Adam took the chair she'd vacated.

"I'm glad you're over here where it's quiet," he said. "I want to talk to you."

Maureen kept her attention firmly on the plate in her lap. She didn't want to talk to him. At least, not in a personal way. "Why aren't you eating?" she asked.

"I've already wolfed mine down."

"I didn't know there was going to be a party tonight. You ought to have warned me, and I would've stayed in town for supper."

As Adam studied her lowered head, it dawned on him that she truly felt like an intruder, that her presence here would more than likely be resented. And the memory of her words came back to haunt him again.

My maternal grandmother was the only relative around who was willing to take me in. But she died by the time I was eight. After my grandmother died I was raised in foster homes. I didn't divorce my husband. He left me.

"Why would you do something like that?" he asked. "There's plenty of food for everyone."

"I'm not a member of the family, and this is a family gathering."

Adam wondered if she'd ever felt as if she belonged to any family. Or anyone.

"I'm sure they'll all forgive you for having a different last name."

She lifted her head and looked at him. "You said

you wanted to talk to me. Has something happened at work?''

Adam leaned back against the chair and crossed his ankles out in front of him. ''Actually, something has happened. Dad told me you're going to move into your house in the next day or two. Why didn't you tell me?''

She shrugged as her gaze fell back to her plate. ''I didn't figure it would interest you. After all, you're not any of my business. Remember?''

Adam silently cursed. ''You would bring that up,'' he muttered.

''Why not?'' she said between bites. ''You made a good point. Your private life is off-limits to me. And mine is none of your business. So we're even. Just impersonal co-workers.''

She was right. Or at least she should be, Adam thought. But things weren't that simple between them. He knew it and so did she.

''If you're finished eating, let's take a walk,'' he suggested.

Her head jerked up. ''Why?''

The wariness in her voice annoyed the hell out of Adam. ''Does there have to be a reason? I'd just like for you to go for a walk with me.''

She studied him with wry speculation, and then with a negligent shrug, she rose to her feet. ''All right. Let me dump my leftovers.''

He quickly left the chair and took the paper plate and cup from her hands. ''I'll do it for you.''

She waited on the porch while he carried the things over to a plastic trash barrel. When he returned, he took hold of her elbow and guided her out in the courtyard among his milling relatives.

For the next twenty minutes, Maureen met aunts, uncles, cousins and second cousins. Each one greeted her warmly and she was genuinely moved at their efforts to make her feel welcome. Yet it was Adam himself who touched her the most. Not necessarily by anything he said to her or even because his hand remained on her arm the whole time. She was struck by the enormous amount of love that shone in his eyes for his family.

"Where are we going now?" she asked as he urged her away from Rose and toward the courtyard gate.

"I told you we were going for a walk."

The fact that he'd made a point of introducing her to his family had already surprised her. She figured he didn't care whether she knew his relatives or not. And now a walk? She cut him a skeptical glance. "I thought we just did."

Adam laughed. "Thirty feet across the backyard is not what I call a walk."

Outside the gate, the two of them passed a row of parked vehicles, then headed down the dirt lane leading away from the house.

"I don't understand the purpose of this," Maureen went on. "Do I look as if I need to walk off a few pounds or something?"

Adam glanced down at her as they strolled along in the falling twilight. Even the loose blue blouse she was wearing couldn't hide the alluring curves of her figure.

"You don't look like you've gained weight, if that's what you want to hear," Adam told her.

"What I want to hear is why we're on this little jaunt," she retorted. From the moment he'd walked up to her on the porch, she'd been leery of his motives. Maybe because she knew he had the power to hurt her.

"You've been avoiding me again. I thought we were going to be friends."

She sighed as she glanced over at the tall pines lining the edge of the road. It was hard for Maureen to imagine he expected her to forgive and forget his cutting remarks.

"I tried to tell you I didn't think it would be possible for us to be friends."

"And why do you think that is? Because you know each time I'm near you I want to touch you? Or that you want to touch me?"

With a loud gasp, she stopped dead in her tracks and turned to face him. "Are you crazy?" she asked hoarsely.

He nodded. "I've been pretty much crazy since the day I walked into my father's office and saw you there."

So had Maureen, but she hadn't wanted to admit it. Even to herself.

"I don't know why you're telling me any of this. It won't—"

His hand clamped around her upper arm and he tugged her off the road and into a dark stand of pines. The heavy scent of them filled her nostrils as she tilted her head back to look up at him.

"Maybe it's because I'm tired of suffering in silence," he said roughly. "Maybe it's because I'm taking back that stupid promise not to make love to you!"

Her mouth fell open and she spluttered, "You're *not* going to make love to me!"

His mouth twisted tauntingly as he searched her

shocked features. And then without warning, his hand cupped her chin and he lowered his mouth to hers.

Maureen could see what was coming, but her brain refused to do anything about it. As soon as his hand touched her face, she was lost, and everything inside her went still except for the wild beating of her heart.

The feel of his hard lips against hers was just as she remembered and the sweet familiarity melted the last bit of resistance inside her. With a reluctant groan deep in her throat, she slid her arms up and around his neck and arched her body into his. Adam's arms slipped around her waist and gathered her even more tightly against him.

Like a hungry man, he feasted on every contour of her lips until the growing heat inside him demanded more. His tongue delved into the warmth of her mouth and past the sharp edges of her teeth while his hands moved up her rib cage and cupped around both breasts.

Maureen knew it was crazy to let him touch her this way and even more insane to respond to it, but her senses were drugged with desire and for once she didn't want to fight it. She wanted to let herself feel like a woman. *Be* a woman.

"See what I mean?" he whispered roughly when he finally lifted his head and buried his face in the side of her neck. "You want me as much as I want you."

A shudder of longing rippled down her spine and she clutched his shoulders even tighter as her knees grew weak. "That doesn't make it right," she murmured.

His thumbs rubbed across the tips of her breasts

and she squeezed her eyes shut against the onslaught of sensations rushing over her.

"Why isn't it right?" he asked. "We're both adults. And single. Who are we hurting?"

"Each other," she whispered.

He lifted his head, then his hands came up to frame her face as he looked into her eyes. "How can you say that, Maureen?"

She shook her head as a lump formed in her throat. Never had she wanted any man the way she wanted Adam. Yet she wasn't stupid. He wanted nothing to do with love or marriage. He was simply out for physical gratification.

"I don't know what you think of me, Adam. But I don't have affairs."

Adam groaned. "I haven't asked you to have an affair."

Doubt and confusion filled her eyes. "Then what are you asking from me, Adam? Love? Marriage?" Her low laugh was full of bitterness. "I'm not a fool, Adam. I know the sort of man you are."

His nostrils flared. "What sort of man am I?"

"A playboy."

His hands dropped from her face and clamped down on her shoulders. "I'm not—"

"What's the point of trying to deny it?" she interrupted. "Even your family talks about your playing the field."

"Okay," he said, his voice hoarse with frustration. "Maybe I have been a bit of a playboy in the past. But tell me this, Maureen. Since you came here, have you seen me with a woman?"

After a moment's thought, she was forced to shake her head. "No. But it wouldn't matter if I had. I don't have a connection or sole right to you! You wouldn't want me to have one!"

He groaned again as the sense of her words warred with the need in his body. Never had any woman left him so torn and confused, so crazy with need.

"But we do have a connection," he argued. "You know it, and I know it."

She groaned and turned her back to him. "If you're calling this a connection, then you're confused. What we shared a moment ago was lust. Nothing more."

One of his hands meshed in her hair. The other curled around the warm flesh of her upper arm. "Is that what you think?" he murmured.

It wasn't. But she was trying hard to make herself believe it. The last thing she wanted to imagine was that she was falling in love with this man.

"Yes. And if you don't—"

She stopped as his hand propelled her back to him and she faced his searching green eyes. "I don't," he whispered. "I'm not at all sure what I'm feeling for you, Maureen. I just know you make me crazy and I don't want us to be apart."

He was treading on dangerous ground and Maureen was more than tempted to follow him. But the pain of the past kept rearing up inside her, begging her to listen to her head rather than her heart.

"This is getting us nowhere, Adam. You don't even know what you want from me," she said, then her eyes narrowed as she searched his face. "Or maybe you do?"

He frowned. "What is that supposed to mean?"

She drew in a deep breath, then slowly released it. "That you know exactly what you want. You just don't want to come out and say it."

"Say what?"

"That you want me to sleep with you."

Her blunt answer knocked him sideways. His lips parted and all he could do was stare at her in the waning light.

"Well?" she prodded. "Am I wrong?"

"I told you I'm not asking you to have an affair," he said crossly.

"No. You don't want anything that involved. A one-night fling is probably all you want."

Pure frustration had him turning away from her and raking a hand through his hair. "You know I'd be lying if I said I didn't want to make love to you. I made that pretty obvious a moment ago, didn't I?"

Even though he wasn't looking at her, a hot blush stung her cheeks. "Yes, you did. And I—well, I wasn't exactly resisting, either. That's why we need to stay away from each other."

He whirled back around and pinned her with dark eyes. "Why are you making this all so difficult?"

She swallowed as tears stung her throat. She wanted this man. Why couldn't she simply take what he was offering and enjoy the physical pleasure he could give her? she asked herself. As a woman, wasn't she entitled to that much?

Not when her heart would be involved, a little voice inside her answered.

"Because I have to," she answered in a choked voice, then before he could stop her, she hurried out of the pines and back to the narrow dirt road.

"Maureen! Damn it, wait!"

Desperate to get away from him now, Maureen ducked her head and began marching back in the direction of the house. She'd taken four long strides when he caught her from behind.

The grip of his hands on her waist filled her with panic. Not because she was afraid of him, but of herself. She was terrified the reckless emotions roiling around inside her would finally win and she'd throw herself back in his arms. Beg him to make love to her.

"Don't run off like this," he pleaded, his voice rough with anguish.

"I have to," she whispered.

"Why? Why do you have to run from me? Was your husband so awful to you that you're afraid of men? Of me?"

She lifted her head but didn't look at him. Instead, she stared blankly at the mountains rising up in the distance as she remembered David's cold accusations, his total rejection. It had been easy for him to walk away from her and their marriage. So easy that she'd known he'd never really loved her.

When she spoke, her voice was hollow. "My husband didn't physically abuse me. If that's what you mean."

"Then what—"

Her head twisted quickly around and she cut him a mocking glance over her shoulder. "Remember, Adam? We've all had demons in our past. Just like you, I prefer to keep mine locked up."

His lips twisted to a thin, scornful line. "What do you want me to do? Pour out every blasted thing that's ever happened to me?"

Like a bolt of lightning, anger suddenly slashed through her. "I don't want you to do anything but leave me alone!'' She jerked loose from his grasp and began walking.

Adam was forced to follow. ''I can't do that. I've already tried.''

''Then try harder!'' she practically shouted.

They walked the remaining distance to the house in silence, but once there, Adam took her by the arm and urged her toward the front entrance. ''I'm not finished talking to you,'' he said when she shot him a questioning glance.

Dear heaven, hadn't he said enough, done too much already? she wondered wildly.

''Well, I'm finished,'' she said as they entered the quiet living room. Apparently, the crowd of relatives was content to remain outside in the courtyard.

Ignoring her statement, he said, ''I want to know when you're planning on moving.''

At least he'd asked her something she could answer easily. ''The moving van with my things from Houston should be here tomorrow. So this will probably be my last night here at the ranch.''

He winced inwardly at the news, then quickly told himself he shouldn't let her leaving get to him. He'd be going to his own house soon anyway. But he knew his evenings weren't going to be the same without her around.

''I'll help you with your unpacking,'' he told her suddenly.

She immediately shook her head. ''That isn't necessary. The movers will unload the truck and later I can put things away at my own leisure.''

''You'll have boxes everywhere. You don't want to have to live in a big mess for several days,'' he argued.

True, she could use his help, Maureen thought. But after what just happened between them, she'd be crazy to be alone with him again.

"I don't know, Adam, I—"

He threw up his hands in a conciliatory gesture. "I promise I won't lay a finger on you. I'll simply be there to offer my help."

Could she trust him? she wondered. Or more important, could she trust herself?

What are you thinking, Maureen? a voice inside her screamed. *You have to trust the man. You have to work with him. You have to get over this obsessive desire for him or you're going to make a fool of yourself.*

With a sigh of surrender, she said, "All right, Adam, I'll accept help from you. But nothing else. Understand?"

Adam understood only too well. She didn't want to get involved with him in any way for any reason, and the knowledge cut him to the bone.

Trying not to sound as wounded as he felt, he said, "Perfectly. You can keep yourself wrapped safely in ice. You won't find me trying to melt it!"

He brushed on past her, and as Maureen watched him leave the room, a bitter laugh lodged in her throat. *Oh, Adam,* she silently wailed, *don't you know you've already melted my heart?*

Chapter Seven

Maureen stood in the middle of the living room, staring bewilderedly at the mound of boxes stacked on both sides of her. She hadn't remembered having this much junk in her apartment back in Houston.

From the looks of this room alone, Adam had been right, she thought. She needed help. But so far today, she'd neither seen nor heard from the man. Before she'd left the Sanders building that evening, Maureen had briefly considered dropping by his secretary's office to see if he was in, but she'd decided against it. The last thing she wanted was for Adam to think she was chasing him.

Oh, well, she told herself, it really didn't matter whether Adam showed up or not. She would eventually get all these things put away. Besides, it was probably for the best he wasn't here. After last night, she didn't know what to expect from him, or herself. The one thing she did know was that she'd have to get a grip on her emotions or she was going to wind up in love with the man.

The sound of a slamming door interrupted her worried thoughts and she walked over to the front door and peered out. In spite of all her earlier misgivings, her heart clenched at the sight of Adam climbing up the stone steps to the front of the house.

Like last night, he was dressed in jeans and boots and a black T-shirt. Nestled in the crook of one muscular arm was a large grocery sack. But it was the grin on his face that caught Maureen's real interest. She'd expected his anger from their argument last night to still be with him. It was a pleasant surprise to see she was wrong.

"Did you think I'd forgotten?" he asked.

She opened the door and ushered him inside. "I thought you weren't coming," she confessed.

"I had to go to Eunice this morning and just got back less than an hour ago," he explained, then looking around the room, he let out a low whistle. "Boy, you really do need help! Are you a pack rat?"

Maureen's soft laugh drew his eyes back to her. She was wearing white leggings and a long, loose top of pink-and-white stripes. Her hair was twisted into a loose knot and clamped at the back of her head with a large tortoiseshell barrette. Pink tinged her cheeks and lips, and Adam decided she couldn't have looked more beautiful if she'd been wearing diamonds and furs.

"I didn't think so until I walked through the house and looked at all the boxes." She sniffed the air as smells from the paper bag in his arm began to permeate the room. "Is that food?"

He nodded. "Have you eaten yet? I stopped by a deli before I started out here."

She motioned for him to follow her into the kitchen area. "No. I didn't take time," she told him. "The moving van was here and I wanted to make sure all the large pieces of furniture were put in the right rooms before the men left."

Adam placed the sack down on the countertop and began pulling out an assortment of luncheon meats, breads, cheeses, accompanying condiments and cold cans of soda. "I brought paper plates and plastic utensils, too. Just in case you hadn't found yours yet."

"Actually, I've found the dishes, but I need to line the shelves before I put them in the cabinets."

She helped him carry the groceries over to an oak dining table set in a small alcove off the kitchen. As she took a seat across from him and they began to make sandwiches, Adam looked curiously out the window.

"This is a beautiful place, but don't you think you'd feel a little safer in town?"

She cast him a vague smile. "I'll feel safe enough. And anyway, I'd like to get a dog. A big outside dog. Like a Doberman pinscher."

He chuckled with dismay as he piled cold cuts and cheese atop a slice of sourdough bread. "You don't want a dog, you want a killer."

Maureen wrinkled her nose at him. "Not at all. Dobermans are sweet, affectionate animals. I had a friend who lived in the country who had one. I loved it."

Adam cut her a sly glance. "Was this friend a male?"

"The dog friend or the human friend?" she asked.

"The human friend."

"It was a married couple, actually. He'd retired from the same gas company I worked for in Houston."

"Oh. I thought it might have been a young, handsome friend."

Her expression dour, she shook her head. "I told you, Adam. I don't date."

"Are you telling me you haven't dated since your divorce?"

She popped the lid off the soda can and took a long swallow. "That's exactly what I'm telling you."

She wasn't yet thirty and she was beautiful and sexy. Why was she wasting her life? he wondered. But then he had to remind himself that he, too, had turned his back on love.

"Then I'm afraid my parents are in for a difficult task."

She glanced at him sharply. "What are you talking about?"

He swallowed a bite of sandwich, then said with a measure of sarcasm, "They want to introduce you to some eligible bachelors."

Maureen's sandwich stopped midway to her mouth. "I hope you're kidding."

"They think you're lonely."

Lonely. Adam or any of his family couldn't know what the past few years of her life had been like. Many nights she'd deliberately worked herself to the point of exhaustion just so she wouldn't have to go home and face an empty apartment.

She figured many people would probably say she had only herself to blame for her solitary existence. But none of them really knew or understood what she'd gone through with David. Maybe a stronger woman could have forgotten and moved on. But so far, Maureen hadn't found the courage.

"Don't your parents realize there are other hobbies besides the opposite sex?"

"No. They've been deliriously in love for twenty-five years."

Maureen forced herself to take another bite of her sandwich. As she chewed, she studied Adam's grim expression. He appeared to be far more disturbed about his parents' plan to find her a love interest than she did.

"You're their son. Why aren't they focusing on finding you the right partner?"

His lips turned down at the corners as he reached for his soda. "Because they've given up on me."

Why? Maureen desperately wanted to ask. But she kept the one word inside her. It would never do for them to keep harping on this subject.

"Well, it's very nice of them to be concerned about me. But they'll soon learn I'm just not interested."

Last night, she'd kissed him as though she was more than interested, Adam thought. But he wasn't going to point that out to her right now. He was here to help her unpack, not to seduce her.

Darkness had fallen by the time they finished their simple meal. While Maureen put the leftovers away in the refrigerator, Adam went through the house, turning on lights and stacking boxes to one side so they could have clear walking paths.

They started in the kitchen by lining shelves and putting away dishes, utensils and pots and pans. Maureen was surprised at Adam's understanding of where things should go and how the working order of the room should be laid out. She hadn't expected him to know about such things, and he laughed when she told him so.

"I'm a man of many talents," he assured her with a cocky grin. "You're going to realize that once you really get to know me."

She climbed down from her perch on the counter-top and dusted her hands against the sides of her thighs. "I'm about to see how good you are in the interior decorating department," she told him, then asked, "Do you have any patience at all?"

"I was standing behind a door when God was handing out patience."

She chuckled. "Well, I'll try not to test the little you have. I only need you to hang a few pictures on the wall."

"Hang pictures! Woman, are you crazy? You've got dozens of boxes to unpack and you're worried about hanging pictures?"

She gave him a mocking smile. "Already trying to get out of the job?"

He shook his head as though he'd never understand women, then motioned her out of the kitchen. "If we're finished in here, we'd better get started or we'll never make it to work by eight in the morning."

As it turned out, hanging Maureen's oil paintings and watercolors didn't take as long as Adam first expected. In no time, the two of them had also cleared out the boxes in the living room and arranged the furniture and lamps into a comfortable setting.

"Are you sure this is the way you want every-thing?" Adam asked as they stood back and surveyed the long room.

"Yes. I like it. Don't you?"

He glanced at her with dismay. "Yes. But I figured you'd want to change your mind at least two or three times before we called it quits in here."

She frowned at him. "I'm not a fickle woman. Once I make up my mind about something, it stays that way."

Adam's expression grew serious as he searched her brown eyes. "Does that include me?"

"What does that question mean?" she asked warily.

He wanted to close the two steps between them. He wanted to take her into his arms, pull the clasp from her hair and kiss her lips until neither one of them could think about the right or wrong of it.

"Have you really made up your mind to keep your hands off me?"

She turned away from him quickly but not before Adam caught a glimpse of torment on her face. "I thought we went all through this last night. You told me you wouldn't—"

"I'm not going to try anything with you," he interrupted sharply. "I just thought…" He stopped and shook his head with self-disgust. "Hell, I don't know why I even want you to change your mind."

She twisted around to face him and he could see her eyes were filled with anguish. "I don't know why, either. I'm sure there are all sorts of women out there who'd be more than willing to have an affair with you."

An affair. The word had never really seemed distasteful to Adam before. Playing the field had always seemed the natural thing for him to do. But now, when Maureen merely said the word *affair*, he inwardly cringed. "I don't want to just bed a woman, Maureen."

She groaned and shook her head. "You don't want love or marriage, either, Adam. So what's left? What do you want?"

I want you. The realization struck him with such force he could only stare at her.

"That's exactly what I thought," she went on before he could make any sort of reply. "You're out for a good time. And that's all."

Frowning with disgust, he said, "You really think poorly of me, don't you?"

She forced herself to smile and lighten the tension that had been building for the past few moments. "No. Just wisely," she said, then motioned for him to follow her.

Adam had helped her unpack several boxes of clothes and shoes when Maureen decided she would go to the kitchen and put on a pot of coffee. While she was gone, Adam opened the last two boxes marked Miscellaneous and began to place the items out on the bed so Maureen could see what else she had to find storage space for.

There was a small cedar jewelry box, several clumps of silk flowers, an assortment of vases and a collection of old college textbooks, all of which were on the subject of geoscience. In the second box, he found several more books, most of which were best-selling fiction. As he sifted through the paperbacks, he expected to find at least one romance, but he didn't.

When Maureen had sworn off love, she must have well and truly meant it, he thought.

With the books piled out of the way, he found two

photo albums, but as soon as he realized what they were, he closed the covers and placed them aside. He didn't know anyone in Maureen's past, so he wouldn't recognize who or what was in the photos. Besides, he felt to look at them would be invading her privacy. And he respected her too much to do that.

Beneath the albums, at the bottom of the box, was a small, hand-sewn quilt with cats and dogs embroidered on each square. Adam didn't know anything about quilts, but he was pretty sure this one was some sort of baby blanket and he wondered if it was something she'd hung on to from her tragic childhood.

He lifted the quilt out of the box, and as he did so he realized something was wrapped inside it. He laid the colorful blanket out on the bed, then carefully unfolded it. Inside was a small yellow baby rattle and a gold-framed photo of a very small baby girl. At the bottom, a lock of dark hair was captured beneath the glass.

He was studying the baby's features, trying to figure out whether the picture was of Maureen, when he heard her footsteps enter the room. Still holding on to the photo, he glanced at her. "Is this adorable baby girl you?" he asked with a grin.

She didn't smile. In fact, her face had a frozen look as she stepped over to him.

"No. It's not me," she said curtly. She reached out to take the photograph from him, but he kept a grip on it.

"Then who is it?" he asked. "You told me you didn't have any close relatives. She must belong to a friend."

"It doesn't matter."

"The child is obviously important to you," he persisted. "Why don't you want to tell me who she is?"

Maureen reached up and tugged the frame from his hand, then pressed the photograph facedown to her bosom. Her features were stiff when she finally spoke. "The baby was my daughter, Elizabeth."

The words hit him like a fist in the face. "Your daughter!"

She nodded and turned away from him. Adam stared at her rigid back as all sorts of questions whirled through his mind.

"You said *was* your daughter. Where is she now? With her father?" Had the man who'd walked out on Maureen also taken their child from her, too? Just the thought made Adam want to hunt the man down and kill him.

The sound that slipped out of her was choked and bitter. "No. My daughter is dead."

Adam didn't know what to say. What to think. She'd never once mentioned having a child. Or losing one.

For long moments, he stood in stunned silence as he pictured her going through the pain and joy of birth, then later the utter grief of having the baby taken from her.

Slowly, he closed the small space between them and placed his hands on her shoulders. "Tell me," he whispered.

Shaking her head, she refused to look at him.

"Tell me," he urged again, bringing his cheek against hers.

His closeness gave her the strength to swallow down the tight knot of tears in her throat and finally she was able to say, "I can't, Adam."

"How long has it been since you lost her?"

"Ten years." She drew in a bracing breath. "Elizabeth died of crib death. She wasn't quite three months old."

"Oh, Maureen."

It was all he said, yet it was enough for her to feel his sympathy. In fact, his stark response was far better than those she'd received directly after she'd lost Elizabeth. Many had tried to console her with medical explanations for her baby's death and then there'd been others who'd urged her to forget her lost child and have another to replace her. Maureen had wanted to scream that a child could never be replaced.

"I was still in college when it happened," she found herself saying. "David was putting in long hours as an electrician's helper. And I was...well, I was determined to finish my master's. It was my last semester and I was studying for final exams. I had moved the baby's crib into the kitchen so I could watch her while I studied at the dining table. David came in later that night and found me sound asleep with my head on an open book. Elizabeth was...she wasn't breathing."

"So your husband was still living with you at the time?"

She nodded, then slowly turned to face him. There was such a look of utter desolation on her face that Adam felt as if he'd been kicked in the chest by a wild horse.

"Yes, we were still married at the time. But he left a few days after Elizabeth's funeral. He...well, he believed I was selfish and negligent. He accused me of putting my career before my baby. He said if I'd been taking care of Elizabeth like a real mother instead of sticking my nose in a damn textbook, she wouldn't have died."

Adam's head reared back in total disbelief. "No," he said quietly. "I can't believe that, Maureen. The man must have been crazy."

Her gaze dropped to the floor between their feet. "Logically, I knew he was wrong. But emotionally, I already felt guilty about Elizabeth's death. David took pleasure in driving the guilt even deeper."

Adam shook his head as he tried to fathom the heartbreak and loss Maureen must have suffered. How had she managed to hold up under it? he wondered.

"How could he have said such things? Anyone with any sense knows crib deaths are unexplainable. Even if you watched the baby every second of the day and night, the vigil still wouldn't have necessarily saved her life," he reasoned.

"Like I said, logically, I understood all that. But I was so wounded and full of grief I had to blame someone, and I was the one who was taking care of her."

"Is that why he left you? Because of the baby?"

Maureen tilted the picture away from her chest and stared down at the child she'd given birth to. In some ways, losing her seemed so long ago. Yet the pain was still as sharp and fresh as if it had happened yesterday.

"Elizabeth's death gave him a reason to turn his back on me."

"He couldn't have loved you, Maureen. A real husband would've been there for you to lean on and he would've needed to lean on you. The man must have been a real bastard."

"It was my fault for not having realized his true feelings about me before I married him," she said with bitter resolution.

"Did you love him?" Adam had to ask.

She let out a weary sigh. "When I first started dating David, he showed me more attention than I'd ever had in my life. And I guess...I mistook his physical affection for real love."

"But did you love him?" he repeated.

She glanced away from him. "I thought I did. I married him with hopes and plans for a family and a future. But that...didn't happen."

She carried the picture over to a long cherry wood dresser and placed it in a bottom drawer. Adam picked up the baby quilt and rattle and crossed the room to her. "Do you want to put these things with the photo?" he asked.

She took the items from him, and Adam couldn't help but notice her fingers trembled as she absently traced the outline of a sleeping cat.

"I guess you must think I'm a pretty horrid mother," she said huskily. "For putting my daughter's picture completely out of sight."

He watched her fold the quilt into a small square and place it and the rattle in the same drawer with the photo.

"No. I think you loved her so much you can't bear to see her little face every day."

That he understood so completely startled Maureen. Her gaze flew up to his and she studied his drawn features with wet, grateful eyes. "I did love her, Adam. More than my very life. After I lost my parents and grandmother, I had no family. I grew up not knowing what it was like to have a brother or sister. A mommy or daddy. And I vowed I would someday have a family and children of my own. But…''

She stopped and shrugged as though she had come to accept the deal fate had handed her. ''Losing Elizabeth and my husband was the final blow. The whole thing proved it wasn't meant for me to have anyone.''

Adam could no longer bear it. He tugged her into his arms. Thankfully, she didn't resist, and he drew her cheek against his shoulder and stroked his fingers gently down the middle of her back.

''You're still young enough, Maureen. You could find a husband and have more children.''

''So I could lose them, too?'' she asked, her brittle voice muffled by the folds of his T-shirt. ''Just like I lost my mother and father? My granny? My husband and baby?'' She shook her head back and forth against his shoulder. ''No. I can't go through that sort of grief again. I'd rather be alone for the rest of my life.''

So now he knew, Adam thought sadly. She'd not only lost her daughter, she'd also been betrayed by a man whom she'd undoubtedly loved. The hurt had been too much for her to forget. And because he understood so completely, his heart ached for her. Everything inside him made him want to hug her fiercely to him, assure her that she wasn't put here on earth to be punished.

''Someday you're going to wake up and be sorry you feel that way, Maureen.''

She tilted her head back to look at him. ''Like you? You're not sorry.''

Oh, yes, he was very sorry, he suddenly realized. He wished with every fiber of his being that he could get past Susan's death. He wished he could open his heart and say, "I love you, Maureen. Be my wife. Bear my children." But he couldn't. He'd learned life was too fragile, too unpredictable, to risk his heart a second time.

"I guess you're right, Maureen," he said dismally.

She pulled away from him, carefully dabbed at her eyes and blinked back the remaining tears. "It's getting late and we still have several more boxes of things to put away. We're not getting anywhere like this."

No. And they never would, Adam thought grimly. Maureen was too embittered to let herself love again. And he was simply too afraid. So what was he doing here with this woman? Why did he still ache to hold her, comfort her, love her?

Love her. Love her. Had he already fallen in love with Maureen and he just didn't know it?

Adam wouldn't allow himself to answer that question.

Chapter Eight

Adam dropped the telephone receiver on its cradle and leaned wearily back in his leather office chair. Nothing seemed to be going right anywhere.

A tool pusher on a rig in Bloomfield had suddenly quit without warning. An electrical fire had destroyed several generators and injured two men on another rig in Louisiana, and now an outraged landowner in Oklahoma was threatening their crew of seismograph workers with a shotgun to stay clear of his property. It didn't matter that the oil company had already paid the man a hefty right-of-way fee. He was determined to kill someone or see Sanders Gas and Exploration in court.

Rubbing the dull ache in his temples, Adam turned his chair toward the plate-glass wall overlooking the mountains. Black clouds were beginning to gather over the distant peaks for their daily afternoon shower.

As he absently watched the clouds grow darker, his

thoughts turned to Maureen. Not that she was ever really far from his mind. There was rarely a waking minute of the day he wasn't thinking about her and wondering what he going to do about his obsession with the woman.

And that's what it was, he thought crossly. An obsession, a fixation he couldn't get over.

Since the night he'd helped her move into her house, he'd seen her only briefly. She'd been buried in the lab during the day, and now that she was no longer staying on the Bar M, he had no chance of seeing her in the evenings.

Which was probably all for the best, he thought wearily. Since she'd told him about her baby, he couldn't stop aching for her. More than anything, he wanted her to be happy. But he didn't know how to help her. She'd already grieved for ten years. He was probably crazy to think he could put a stop to her sorrow.

A knock at the door interrupted his musing. Not bothering to pull his boots from the corner of the desk, he called, "Come in."

"Are you busy, honey?"

Adam turned his head in time to see his mother entering the room. She was wearing a dress and her red hair was wound in an elaborate twist at the back of her head. She looked particularly beautiful, and in spite of his mood he couldn't help but smile at the sight of her.

"Hi, Mom. What are you doing in town? Shopping?"

She laughed and waved away his words. "Not hardly. The only place I usually shop in is the feed store and I can do that in a pair of jeans."

He motioned toward her classy black dress. "So what are you up to? You and Dad got a hot date?"

She smiled impishly. "Something like that. Your father and I are going to fly down to El Paso this evening to meet with that oilman from Port Arthur. Wyatt's promised to take me dancing afterward."

"That's nice."

She walked over and leaned her hip against the edge of his desk. "Would you like to come with us?"

He glanced up at her. "No. You two don't need my company. Besides, I've had a rough day."

"You look awful," she said, her voice full of concern.

Frowning, Adam rose from his chair and walked over to the wide expanse of glass. "Thanks, Mom. That makes me feel much better."

She sighed, but it was so low Adam didn't hear it. "Actually, I'm here with an invitation from your aunt Justine. She's giving Rose and Harlan an anniversary party Saturday night. It's their twenty-fifth."

"I may have to go out of town," he said. "There's some trouble brewing with some lease land in Oklahoma. But I'll go if I'm here."

"Good. I'll tell her to count you in if at all possible. Now about Maureen. Do you want to invite her, or shall I?"

He cut his mother a sharp glance. "Mother, we barely managed to get the woman to stick around for Miguel's birthday party. I seriously doubt she'd want to come to another of our family gatherings."

"Nonsense," Chloe said with a wave of her hand. "I'm sure she'll be glad for an excuse to get out of the house. Besides, some of Roy's young deputies might be there. And if her taste doesn't run to lawmen, there'll be a few cowboys who might catch her eye."

It was all Adam could do to keep from cursing a blue streak. "Why in hell can't you leave Maureen alone, Mother? She doesn't want a man!"

Chloe's brows peaked with skepticism as she studied her son's moody face. "How do you know she doesn't want a man?"

"I just do," he barked.

"Oh, I don't know why I bother with you," she muttered. "You've always got a thorn in your side these days!"

"Where are you going?" Adam demanded as she started out the door.

Chloe peered at him from the open doorway. "I'm going down to the lab to give Maureen the invitation myself. It appears to be too much of a problem for you."

"Damn it, just stay away from the lab! I'll ask Maureen about the party mself."

"Well, I hope it doesn't put too much of a strain on you," she retorted. Then before a grin could appear on her face, she quickly stepped into the hall and slapped a hand over her mouth to stifle her chuckle.

When Adam walked into the lab a couple of hours later that evening, Maureen was studying a small portion of shale with her naked eye. The moment she realized he was in the room, she straightened to her full height and pushed her fist against the small of her back.

"Wouldn't a microscope tell you more?" he asked.

"Not always," she said.

Since the night he helped her move, she hadn't

talked to him. She didn't know if he'd simply been busy with work or deliberately avoiding her. She was beginning to think he'd had second thoughts about her now that he knew about Elizabeth's death. Maybe he'd decided she really was a selfish career woman.

"I haven't seen you all week. I was starting to think you'd buried yourself in here," he said.

"I've had a lot of tests to run," she explained, but she wasn't being entirely truthful. She could have left the lab on several occasions, but each time she'd stopped herself.

Every moment she was in Adam's company, she knew she was losing a little bit more of her heart. She couldn't trust herself to see him every day, even though everything inside her wanted to be with him.

"Is your house the way you want it now?" he asked as his eyes took in the rich color of her brown eyes, the faint splash of scarlet across her cheekbones and the ruby red of her lips. A little more than two hours ago, he was agonizing over what to do about this woman. But now, oddly enough, his mother's innocent remark had ended his turmoil. He knew what he wanted and he'd decided what he had to do.

Maureen flexed her tired shoulders. "Almost."

"And you like it?" he asked.

This week as she'd puttered around the rooms, hanging curtains and tinkering with decorations, Maureen had slowly come to the realization the house just wasn't the same without him in it. Yet she knew she couldn't let him know how she felt. He'd see her admission as a green light, and before she knew what was happening, she'd be in bed with him.

With a wry smile, she walked over to a metal chair at one end of a worktable and took a seat. "It's not a home like the Bar M. But it's enough for me." It had to be, she told herself.

Adam moved over to where she was sitting and rested his hip against the edge of the table. "I'm glad," he said, and meant it. More than anything, he wanted her to be happy.

As Maureen studied his handsome profile, she could feel her heart begin to throb more rapidly. And she wondered how long it would be before she could look at this man without wanting him. Days? Months? Or would she never get over the incessant need to touch him, to be near him?

"What about your house?" she asked. "How much longer do the carpenters think they'll need?"

"Another week and I'll be able to move back in."

Her brows arched with surprise. "Really? Those two men must really work fast."

He watched her finger make an invisible line on the tabletop, and as he did he was suddenly remembering the feel of her hands against his face, the gentleness of her touch, the softness of her skin.

"I, uh, decided to take your advice and not do anything else to the house. It would've been a waste of time and money."

He couldn't have shocked her more, and her lips parted as she stared at him. "Oh, Adam, my intentions were not to necessarily change your mind. It's your house. You should change it whatever way *you* want."

Shrugging, he glanced away from her. "I don't know why the hell I was trying to make it feel like home. All I needed was a place to eat and sleep and change my clothes. And anyway, you were right. It would take a wife and children to make it into a home like the Bar M.''

Just as it would take a husband and children to make her house into the home she'd always wanted, she thought sadly. But she wasn't a fool. Even if she was willing to risk her heart again, she knew this man wouldn't or couldn't give her the home she needed.

After several moments passed and she didn't make any sort of reply, he decided it was time to get to the point. He cleared his throat and folded his arms across his chest. "Actually," he began, "the reason I'm here is to give you an invitation."

"Oh? To what?"

"A party. Given by my aunt Justine. It's to celebrate Rose and Harlan's twenty-fifth wedding anniversary."

She quickly shook her head. "I'm not a party person, Adam. And this sounds like another family gathering."

"There'll be other people attending besides family members," he assured her while trying not to think about the single lawmen and cowboys his mother had mentioned. He wasn't about to let one of them so much as glance at her sideways.

"Are you going?" she asked.

"Yes. Unless I have to travel to Oklahoma. Things are getting in a hell of a mess back there. The seismograph crew have been met with a double-barreled shotgun for the past three days they've tried to work."

"Dear heaven, why not get the law to handle things?" she asked. She didn't want to think of Adam getting mixed up in a land-rights feud.

"I'm sure you know things like this can get held

up in court for months on end. I'd rather try to negotiate with the landowner myself. Usually when they see a company man traveling a long distance just to make an effort to deal with them in person, they back down.''

"I hope you're right," she said gravely. "Otherwise, you might be having shotgun pellets dug out of you.''

He chuckled, then as his gaze came to rest on her face, his expression sobered. "Well, you'd probably be relieved to get rid of me.''

I don't have you, she wanted to point out to him. But she kept the words inside her with all the rest of the pain. "I wouldn't like seeing you hurt. Breaking your ankle was bad enough.''

Without warning, he moved closer and cupped his hand around her chin. It was all Maureen could do not to close her eyes and simply savor the feel of his work-roughened skin against her.

"I've been thinking a lot about all the things you told me the other night. About your daughter. And your ex-hus—''

"I try not to think about them, Adam. Please, let's not go into it again," she whispered hoarsely.

He took her by the hand and drew her to her feet. Once she was standing and his gaze was locked with hers, he said, "I'm not going to go into it again, Maureen. I understand the memories cause you pain and I don't want to be the cause of that. I only…I want to know if you believe I'd be like him. Do you think I could hurt you the way he did?''

The last thing she expected from him was such a forthright question, and for long moments she could only stare at him in stunned fascination. "Adam," she finally murmured, "why are you asking me such a thing? It doesn't matter what I believe. Why can't you just let things between us die a natural death?"

His hands came up to frame her face. Gently, his thumbs pressed into her cheeks as he studied her troubled eyes. "Because I—"

The rest of his sentence was left unspoken as the door to the lab opened and a secretary noisily cleared her throat. Choking back a curse, he stepped away from Maureen and turned to face the other woman.

"Is something wrong, Laura?"

She glanced regretfully at her boss. "I'm afraid so, sir. You're needed on the telephone immediately."

He nodded. "I'll be right there."

The young woman scurried out of the lab. At the same time, Maureen crossed the room and began to shuffle through a stack of test reports.

Adam quickly went to her and took hold of her forearm. She glanced at him warily, then back at her work. "Shouldn't you be going?" she asked.

"I am going. I wanted to tell you that we'll finish this later."

This. What was *This?* she wondered wildly. "Adam, I don't—"

"I'll see you later," he promised, then turned and hurried out of the lab.

By the time Maureen had wrapped up most of her day's work and left the building, she had yet to see or hear from Adam again. On the one hand she was greatly relieved. Her emotions had been so raw the past few days she knew she wasn't capable of putting up much resistance where he was concerned. Yet on the other she was troubled by his parting words and the look in his eyes when he'd touched her face. It was a look that said, "I still want to make love to you and I won't give up until I do."

"Maureen, wait!"

Adam's voice froze her hand in midair as she reached out to open the door of her pickup truck. Glancing over her shoulder, she saw him striding quickly across the parking lot to join her.

"I'm on my way home," she said when he drew closer.

He shook his head. "I want to talk to you first. Let's get in my truck and we'll go eat something."

"I have dinner waiting for me in the slow cooker at home," she told him.

"We'll go to your house, then."

She glared at him. "I'm trying to tell you no in a nice way."

He gave her a crooked, tantalizing smile. "I never did like the word *no*. I've pretty much trained my ears not to hear it."

Realizing she was fighting a losing battle, she gestured toward his vehicle. "All right," she said with a groan of resignation. "You can follow me home and I'll feed you some pot roast. But after that, you're going to make a quick exit. I have work to do tonight."

He frowned at her. "Wyatt doesn't expect you to work overtime. Unless it's absolutely necessary."

Wyatt didn't expect her to sleep with his son, either, but that's exactly what was going to happen if they didn't stay away from each other.

"Well, this is necessary," she told him, then climbed into her pickup and shot out of the parking lot.

Apparently, he didn't follow her immediately. As she started climbing the mountain northwest of town, she couldn't spot his vehicle in the rearview mirror and by the time she reached her house, he was still nowhere in sight.

Grateful for the few extra moments to collect herself, she went to the bedroom and quickly changed into a loose cotton dress of burgundy and white flowers, then let down her hair and brushed it loose against her back.

Maureen was placing plates and silverware on the dining table when Adam pulled his truck to a halt at the bottom of her cliffside yard. She met him at the door, her brows lifting suspiciously as he handed her a bottle of wine.

"To go with dinner," he explained.

"What if I changed my mind and decided to give you a piece of bologna instead of pot roast?" she asked wryly.

"Wine goes well with anything," he said softly, and Maureen suddenly knew she had a fight ahead of her.

Adam followed her into the kitchen, where she immediately fetched two long-stemmed glasses from the cabinet and handed them to him.

"Here. Since you brought the wine, you're in charge of serving it. I'm going to make a salad and then we'll be ready to eat."

Adam placed the glasses and the bottle of wine on the table, then walked to the doorway of the kitchen and peered into the living room.

Everything was just as it was when he'd helped her several nights ago. None of the furniture or paintings had been rearranged. Even the lamps were still where he'd placed them. The only difference was that she'd arranged flowers here and there on tabletops and added several bright throw pillows to the couch and overstuffed chairs. At one end of the room, a wall of shelves now bulged with books and knickknacks, while potted plants lined the wide windowsills. It was all very comfortable and inviting. And coupled with the delicious smell of cooked beef, it gave Adam the warm feeling of coming home.

"The house looks very nice," he said as he turned back into the kitchen. "You've been busy."

"This is the first time I've ever owned a house," she admitted. "I like the quietness. And I especially like knowing it's mine and no one else's."

After all she'd been through in her life, Adam could understand her need to have something of her very own, even if it was just a structure of stucco and wood.

Maureen placed the platter of pot roast and accompanying vegetables on the table and they took their seats and began to serve themselves. After Adam had poured the wine and she'd taken a generous sip, she decided to meet him head on instead of prolonging the agony.

"Okay, Adam, what do you want to tell me?"

"Not now. After we eat."

Exasperated, she leaned back in her chair and studied his stoic features. "Why are you doing this to me? I'd planned on enjoying my food tonight. Now I have to eat with a knot in my stomach."

Adam could have told her he'd had a knot in his stomach for the past week. Food was something he ate only to keep his body going and sleep was just a fight with the sheets and pillows until he passed out from exhaustion.

"You really don't trust me, do you?"

She didn't trust herself. Not around him. He had the ability to charm her right out of her senses.

"I'll answer that later. As you're going out the door," she told him.

In spite of the underlying tension between them, they finished the food on their plates and even managed to make casual conversation. Maureen had picked up a rich chocolate dessert from a deli in town the day before and they finished the meal with the sweet and cups of strong coffee.

"Would you like to go outside and look around the place?" she suggested once he'd helped her clear the table. "There's a yard light in the back that pretty well lights up the area around the house."

He agreed and followed her out a sliding glass door and onto a small patio made of red brick. Positioned in one corner was a round table and chairs made of black iron mesh. Otherwise, there was nothing else to be seen except for the thick growth of forest only a few feet away.

"I think I'll get a feeder for the chipmunks and birds," she told him.

He grunted with amusement. "Well, at least you'd give the Doberman something to eat."

She pulled a face at him. "I'm considering getting a cat, too. It might be a menace to the birds, but I can always put a bell around its neck."

She was smiling as she talked and Adam's green eyes warmed as they traveled over her lovely features and long, shiny hair. The fabric of her dress was soft and fluid and caressed her curves like the teasing hand of a lover. Earlier when she'd met him at the door, he'd been blown away by her beauty. He still was.

"You think you need all these animals you're planning on getting for company?"

She glanced away from him but not before he caught a look of warning flicker in her eyes. "I don't necessarily need them to survive. For the past ten years, I've managed to do that all by myself."

"Yeah, but have you been happy?" he asked softly as he took a step closer.

She looked at him, then moved off the edge of the patio and walked over to the twisted branches of a juniper tree. Adam followed, and when she broke off a twig of the evergreen, he caught her hand and lifted it and the green needles to his nose.

"Mmm. Smells like the high country," he mused aloud, then dropping her hand, he slid both arms around her slender waist. "And you smell like a desert flower."

"Adam, don't do this," she whispered in protest, yet she didn't back away. She couldn't. She wanted to feel his strong arms around her and the hard length of his body pressed to hers.

"I have to, Maureen. You're like a drug in my system." He pulled her closer, and Maureen felt something inside her melting as her breasts were crushed against his chest and he bent his head and kissed the bare skin of her shoulder.

"If that's the case, I couldn't be good for you," she murmured as her head reeled with the male scent of him and the sultry pleasure of being cocooned in his arms.

"I don't know what's good for me anymore, Maureen. I once believed I did. I thought everything I wanted out of life was all cut-and-dried. Until you came along.'' He pulled his head back from the curve of her neck and studied the shadows playing across her face. ''Now I have to face the fact that I can't live without you.''

Her breath drew in so sharply it made a hissing noise against her teeth. ''You don't know what you're saying, Adam. And we've been through this thing before. I'm not going to have an affair with you and have my name added to the long list of women you've conquered over the years.''

Sudden anger poured over him like a drenching rain. ''Damn it, there is no long list! I may have dated plenty of women. But I didn't have affairs with them. And anyway,'' he added more gently, ''this isn't about sex. I'm—I'm trying to tell you I'm in love with you.''

This time, Maureen was too stunned to even draw in any sort of breath. In fact, it was long moments before she was capable of making her lungs work.

''No!'' She whirled away from him, but rather than head toward the house, she pushed her way deeper into the thick forest of pine and white-barked aspen.

''Maureen! Come back here before you break your neck!''

When she didn't answer, Adam hurried in after her. It took a few moments for his eyes to adjust to the almost total darkness. Once they finally did, he spotted her behind the trunk of a huge pine. Her head was bent and faint tremors were shaking her shoulders.

''Maureen!'' he said with a groan as he clutched her tightly against him. ''Why did you run from me? Why are you crying?''

She lifted her head and tried to sniff back her tears.

"Because I thought—I truly believed you were the one person who would never lie to me."

"I haven't lied to you!"

"Oh, Adam," she wailed. "You know you don't love me. You love women and the pleasure they can give you. That's all."

"Hell, Maureen! I'm not a teenager. If sex was all I wanted, I could easily get it."

Her face burned at his crude retort. Mostly because she knew it was true. "Yes, but for some reason, you think you want it with me."

"Of course I want it with you! I want *everything* with you! That's the whole damn problem!"

Anger gripped his face and she shook her head miserably. "You look as though love has made you deliriously happy."

His fingers bit into her shoulders. "I didn't ask for this to happen to me, Maureen. And I sure as hell didn't want it to. But I...had to be honest with you. I had to tell you how I feel. Because I truthfully can't see my future without you in it."

Just the idea that Adam might truly love her filled her heart with a strange, bittersweet joy. Yet she couldn't let herself feel more, hope for more. If she did, she'd be crushed a second time.

"You might think you love me now. But don't worry, you'll get over it. David did in record time."

"Don't compare me to that bastard," he warned her.

Her legs were starting to feel like jelly, forcing her to clutch his forearms. "Don't you understand that I have to, Adam? I have to compare him to every man I meet. Otherwise, I'd find myself in deep trouble."

Adam was already in deep trouble. This past week

he'd fought with himself over and over about his feelings for Maureen. He didn't want to love her. He didn't want his heart to hope and plan for a life with her. Because he knew it could all be taken away from him in the blink of an eye. But his heart hadn't listened and now he had to convince her to trust him enough to love him.

"What are you going to do, Maureen? Go through the rest of your life alone and believing that every man is like the one who left you?"

She tried to meet and hold his gaze, but everything inside her was shaking so badly she had to look away. "It's easier to be alone, Adam."

"But is it better? You could have more babies, Maureen. *We* could have children."

His suggestion whipped her face around to his again. "You don't want children! You said so—"

His deep growl halted her protest. "I said a lot of damn things I didn't mean!"

Her eyes widened. "If that's the case, how do I know you mean all this now?"

Sheer frustration made him tilt back his head and stare at the canopy of pine branches stretching above their heads. "Have I ever lied to you? About anything?"

Maureen didn't have to think about his question. She was certain he'd always been truthful with her. At least up until this evening. But now she didn't know. She was afraid to believe he truly wanted to have a family with her. It was too much to accept.

"No. You haven't lied. But..." She dropped her hold on his arms and turned away as tears threatened to choke her.

Adam caught her by the shoulders and pressed her

back against his chest. "But what, Maureen?" he asked, bending his head and pressing his lips close to her ear. "Don't you want more children? Don't you want me? Is that what you're trying to say?"

"You don't understand," she said with an anguished moan. "You don't know what it's like to love someone so much and then—then lose them! How do you think I could bear to go through that again with another child?"

Oh, yes, he thought bitterly, he knew what it was like to lose someone. He hadn't forgotten the utter devastation of having his whole future ripped away from him. But Maureen didn't know about his fiancée's death and he seriously doubted it would make any difference if she did. She was too busy wallowing in her own grief to care about him.

Dropping his hold on her shoulders, he said, "I don't see how you could bear to go through the rest of your life without trying to have another child."

His answer stunned her. By the time she'd gathered herself enough to turn and face him, he was already stepping away from her and heading out of the copse of trees.

"Where are you going?" she called in complete dismay.

"Home to the Bar M. I can see I'm wasting my time here."

She stumbled after him and he paused at the edge of the clearing to wait for her. Once she reached him, her hands clutched the front of his white shirt as her eyes pleaded with him to understand. "I warned you before, Adam. I'm not a woman you should want."

He lifted his hand to her face and his forefinger gently smoothed over her cheekbone, then touched the corner of her lips. "But you are the woman I want, Maureen. And sooner or later I'll have you."

He didn't give her the chance to protest. He walked away before she found the strength to say a word.

Through tear-blurred eyes, Maureen watched him cross the clearing and round the corner of the house, then a few moments later she heard the engine in his truck fire to life. But it was a long time before her trembling legs were strong enough to carry her back inside to the empty rooms she pretended were her home.

Chapter Nine

The evening was warm and lovely. All kinds of delicious foods were spread out on long, beautifully decorated tables and a live band was doing a great job on many of her favorite country-and-western songs, but Maureen really didn't know what she was doing here in the backyard of the Pardee ranch. The last thing she felt in the mood for was a party. Especially one celebrating twenty-five years of marriage. The whole thing mocked the fact that Maureen had barely managed to stay married a year.

But Adam's sister, Anna, had called her earlier in the day, insisting that Maureen come, and the woman had been so warm and insistent she hadn't been able to refuse her.

Now as she stood at the edge of the crowd of dancers, Maureen wished she'd listened to her first instinct and stayed home. She was out of place among these people. They were Adam's family. They would never be hers.

"I'm sorry Adam couldn't be here. You must be lost without him."

Maureen glanced around to see Anna had come to stand beside her in the milling crowd. With raised brows, she studied the other woman. "I'm not—"

Laughing softly, Anna waved away her words. "Oh, don't bother giving me a bunch of excuses. I can see how miserable you are. And since this is a very nice party, Adam has to be the reason for the dismal look on your face."

Maureen didn't know whether to be annoyed or grateful for Anna's insight. "Actually, I was thinking I shouldn't be here."

Smiling wryly, Anna shook her head. "I don't know why not. Mom and Justine went out of their way to make sure there were several single men here tonight."

Maureen grimaced. Since she'd first arrived at the ranch tonight, she'd been bombarded with offers to dance. She'd given in and made several rounds on the concrete patio with a few of the men. Admittedly, all of them had been nice and polite, but she hadn't been affected by even one.

"Your mother and aunt wasted their time," she told Anna. "I'm not interested."

"So I can see. None of them is Adam."

Maureen's hand paused in midair as she lifted a glass of punch to her lips. Casting Anna a sidelong glance, she said, "I'm beginning to think you're more like your twin brother than I ever suspected."

Anna tilted her head back and let out a tinkling laugh and Maureen wondered how it would feel to be a woman like her. Anna was loved utterly by a good, strong man. She had a large family who would always be around to support her. And then there were the children she and Miguel would most surely have in the near future. Maureen couldn't imagine such happiness.

"Yes. I suppose we're more alike than regular siblings. We know each other well. That's why I'm glad he's found you."

Maureen's eyes widened. "Anna, he hasn't *found* me! Not in the way you mean. Your brother and I simply work with each other."

Anna's expression turned to knowing indulgence. "Like I said, I know my brother well. He's fallen for you, and I couldn't be happier about it."

Before Maureen could correct her, Anna's pretty features turned solemn.

"You know, Maureen, for long years now, my brother has been very sad. Not on the outside where everyone can see, but in here."

She tapped her chest, and Maureen's brow puckered with confusion. "He won't talk about his past. At least not to me."

"Not to anybody."

"From what I understand, he's gone through a long list of women," Maureen muttered.

Anna grimaced. "None of them meant anything to him. He—"

She stopped abruptly as Justine quickly approached the two of them. "Excuse me, Anna," she said, "but Maureen is wanted on the telephone. It's Adam calling long distance."

Maureen looked at the older woman with surprise. "Adam wants to talk to me?"

Justine nodded, and Anna cut Maureen a sly

glance. "I guess he couldn't wait until he got back to hear your voice," she said smugly.

Maureen could have told her this was one time she didn't know her twin. "I'm sure it's business," she murmured, then to Justine, "Where do I find the telephone?"

"Come along with me to the house and I'll show you."

Maureen followed her through a back entrance to the house, then through a crowded living room.

"You can use the extension in the bedroom," she told her as she motioned for Maureen to follow her down a long hallway. "I don't think you could hear over the noise in the living room and den." Maureen trailed Justine into a darkened room, where Justine quickly switched on a bedside lamp and gestured toward the phone on the nightstand. "Go ahead. I'll hang up the receiver in the kitchen."

Maureen thanked her, and after Justine had hurried out of the room, she nervously licked her lips and picked up the telephone. "Hello."

"Maureen? What the hell took you so long?"

And this from a man who was supposed to love her? She gritted her teeth and tried not to bite back at him.

"I was outside," she explained. "And the house is so full I had to come back here to the bedroom in order to hear."

"I tried you at home. You said you didn't want to go to my aunt and uncle's party."

She could hear resentment or something akin to it in his voice. Obviously, he didn't like having to work while she had the free time to attend social events, Maureen decided. "But you said you wanted me to go. And anyway, Anna called and practically begged me and I couldn't refuse. Why are you calling?''

The direct question brought him to heel and Adam suddenly realized he'd been behaving like a jealous lover. He'd been away from Lincoln County for nearly five days now and all he'd been able to do was think about her. And miss her. At the moment, he was feeling raw all over.

"I'm not making any headway. The seismograph boys are sitting on their hands wasting time and money. I want you to get your things together and fly out and meet me here tomorrow.''

"Me!" she said with a gasp. Gripping the receiver even more tightly, she sank onto the side of the bed. "Why me? I'm a geologist, not a negotiator!"

"The old man doesn't trust me. He has the idea that we're out to ruin his land. You're the scientist. You can put his mind at ease.''

Maureen snorted. "I doubt he'd believe a scientist any more than he would a company man. But I suppose you're not going to leave me any choice in this matter, are you?''

She sounded none too happy, and Adam knew he hadn't handled this conversation the way he'd first intended. But as he waited for his aunt to bring Maureen to the phone, all sort of images had passed through his mind. Images of Maureen dancing in another man's arms hadn't exactly softened his mood.

"No.''

She let out a long breath as she pictured his strong, handsome face. She wanted to see him so badly it was indecent and even more frightening. "All right. I'll pack a few things tonight and catch the first available flight in the morning.''

"Don't wait on a flight! Charter one. You know which pilot our company uses. Call him tonight," he ordered, then gave her the directions where to meet him once she got to Oklahoma.

"I'll be there as quickly as I can," Maureen assured him. "Is that all?"

"No," he said, then suddenly and unexpectedly his voice grew husky. "I miss you. Like hell."

Maureen's eyes squeezed shut as a lump of emotion filled her throat. She hadn't seen him since the night he told her he loved her. The next morning, he'd left for Oklahoma and she'd had entirely too much time to go over every word, every touch, that had passed between them.

"Maureen? Do you...can you not even admit that you miss me?"

She swallowed and pressed her fingertips against her eyelids. "Of course I miss you," she whispered in a choked voice. For the past five days and nights, she'd ached to feel his arms around her, to hear his voice and see his smile. But that didn't make it right or sensible.

The anguish in her voice stabbed Adam's heart and he knew the time until she was once again by his side would be a living hell.

"But you wished you didn't miss me. Am I right?" he asked bitterly.

"Adam, please, let's not get into this now."

She expected him to argue, but he surprised her by asserting, "You're right. I can't say what I want to say without touching you or looking into your eyes."

"Adam," she responded with a groan, "I—"

"Don't say anything else," he interrupted. "We'll talk tomorrow after you get here."

"All right," she agreed as tears began to sting her eyes. "Good night."

He didn't return her farewell and she was about to hang up when she heard his strained voice. "I love you, Maureen."

Too choked to respond, she let the receiver fall back into its cradle, then dropping her face into her hands, she silently wept. She didn't know how long she sat there on the edge of the bed before she felt a slender arm come around the back of her shoulders.

"Maureen? Has something happened?"

She wiped her eyes and glanced up to see Anna's anxious face peering down at her. "Oh, Anna," she whispered miserably, "I'm afraid...I love your brother."

From his seat in the pickup, Adam watched the black western sky boil like an angry witch's cauldron. Bolts of lightning stabbed the ground like the giant tines of a pitchfork. On the dashboard of his pickup, the radio crackled with static as the broadcaster urged people in Latimer County to be prepared to take cover from the oncoming storm.

Where in hell was she? Adam asked himself for the hundredth time. It would be totally dark soon and she should have been here more than three hours ago. This wasn't New Mexico, where electrical storms and deluges of rain were the most likely summer-weather threat. This was Oklahoma, where deadly tornadoes could develop in an instant. And from the looks of the sky hanging over the mountaintops this evening, the atmosphere was ripe and ready for a twister.

Fear clawed at his insides as he once again reached for the phone on the seat beside him. Several hours had passed since he'd contacted the airport in Oklahoma City. Her plane had landed late but safely, they'd told him. Since then, he'd dialed her cellular number countless times without getting any sort of connection. He could only assume the weather had knocked out a tower and the signal wasn't reaching a foot beyond the hood of his truck, much less over the range of mountains he was sitting in.

Cursing under his breath, he punched off the power to the phone and tossed the instrument back onto the seat. He should never have told Maureen to come, he thought miserably. If something happened to her driving on these mountain roads, he wouldn't want to live.

Rain was hitting her windshield as if someone was sloshing great bucketfuls from the heavens above. With her hands gripping the wheel, Mauren leaned forward and tried to peer past the puny efforts of the wiper blades. On both sides of the highway, the treetops were bending and twisting first one way and then the other, while streaks of lightning lit up the wild sky around her.

Maureen knew she should probably pull over and wait for the rain to ease. But the one stop she'd already made had put her even further behind schedule. No doubt Adam was sitting in his own truck champing at the bit, waiting for her to show up at any moment. She had to keep going on this lonely, deserted highway and hope her sense of direction hadn't failed her.

The moment Adam saw her headlights sweep across the wide, graveled turnoff, he clapped his hat down on his head and jumped out into the pouring rain.

Maureen jammed on her brakes and he was inside the cab before she could kill the engine.

"Where in hell have you been, woman?" he shouted. "Do you realize I've been here for four hours?"

Rain was running off his hat in rivulets and soaking into the plush fabric of the bench seat. His shoulders were soaked and drops of water clung to his cheeks and lips. His green eyes were glazed and Maureen thought he looked like an angry storm all unto himself.

"I'm well aware that I'm late," she said calmly.

"Late! This isn't what I call late! It's—indecent! Do you have any idea what's been going through my mind? I—"

"Are you blind?" she interrupted hotly. His anger was like a rush of gasoline on her smoldering nerves. "In case you haven't noticed, there's been a bit of a storm out there. I couldn't exactly drive the normal speed limit. Or maybe you don't care if I break..." Her words trailed off as his gaze narrowed dangerously on the seat belt strap running between her breasts. "What's the matter? Adam, what are you doing?"

Suddenly, he loomed over her, his fingers tripping the safety lock on the belt. With blazing eyes, he tossed the black strap out of the way and his voice rose above the din of the rain. "I don't ever want to see you wearing one of these damn things again! Ever! Do you hear me?"

He was like a crazy man and she didn't know why. Totally bewildered by his behavior, she stared at him.

"Have you gone mad? I've been driving through winding roads in the pouring rain. Roads, I might add, that I've never traveled before in my life, and you tell me I shouldn't be wearing my seat belt! Adam, I—''

Before she could say another word, he jerked her into his arms. With his face buried in the crook of her neck, he groaned, "Oh, God, Maureen, forgive me for yelling at you. I was so damned frightened. I knew you should've been here hours ago and I could only imagine—I've been out of my mind with worry.''

Tremors shook his arms and she could feel his heart pounding wildly against her cheek. Maureen closed her eyes, stunned by the depth of his fear for her safety.

"I'm sorry, Adam. I didn't mean to worry you, but I've been in a storm ever since the pilot crossed over into Texas. I tried your cellular phone several times, but I couldn't even get a ring. My only choice was to keep driving.''

He eased her head back from his chest and his hand trembled as he reached up and smoothed her tangled hair off her forehead. "I know—I know. It doesn't matter anymore. You're here and you're safe.''

With a needy groan low in his throat, his hands slipped to her face. Maureen's heart lurched into a wild gallop as he smothered her cheeks and forehead, nose and chin with kisses. By the time he turned his attention to her lips, she was clinging to him, frantic for the intimate taste of his mouth.

His kiss was desperate and all-consuming. Maureen was gasping for breath and shaking like a leaf when he finally dragged his lips from hers and buried his face in the long curtain of her hair.

"Promise me, Maureen, promise me you'll never

drive in weather like this again. I don't care if I am waiting for you! And promise me you'll never put on another seat belt!''

She reared her head back far enough to study his face. Anguish filled his green eyes and something far more tender. Something she didn't yet want to believe.

''Adam, you're not making sense. You make this big issue of wanting me to be safe and then—''

''If you can't promise me, I'll get a damn hatchet and hack them out of every vehicle you climb into!''

His harsh warning filled her with fury. ''You're not going to do...''

Her words lodged in her throat as the memory of the day she first met Adam suddenly flashed through her mind. He'd refused to wear his seat belt and she'd argued with him about trying to act like a bullheaded tough guy. As a result, he'd been flung from the Jeep. He could have been killed. But thankfully he'd come away from the accident with only a broken ankle.

''Adam,'' she began again, ''you wouldn't wear your seat belt down in South America. Why?''

His eyes drifted to the rain pelting against the windshield. ''I hate the things.''

''Why?'' she persisted.

He looked back at her and she inwardly cringed at the dark, desolate shadows in his eyes. ''Because they're death traps!''

Maureen knew he wasn't simply repeating the standard argument against seat belts. Something had happened to make him feel this deeply, and she had to find out what it was.

Slowly, she reached up and cradled her palm against his jaw. ''Tell me,'' she urged quietly.

"No."

"You made me tell you about Elizabeth. I didn't want to, but I did." And she had, she realized, because she loved him. Because something inside of her had needed to share the pain with him.

For long moments, Adam's eyes delved into hers and then he let out a long, weary breath. "Someone I knew died in a car accident."

Maureen gently shook her head. "I've been acquainted with several people who lost their lives in car accidents. Their deaths only made me more aware of the need for buckling up."

Agony twisted his features. "But this was…different. This was my fiancée."

Maureen didn't know if her shocked gasp was on the inside or out. "Your fiancée?" she echoed. "You were going to be married?"

His face clouded over as he nodded. "Susan was my high school sweetheart. By the time we reached college, we were planning on getting married. I was going to get my degree in engineering and go into the gas and oil business. She was studying to be an elementary teacher. She loved kids and wanted us to have several."

He paused as his features hardened with bitter regret. Maureen waited for him to go on.

"We had everything planned—our whole lives to look forward to. But it never happened. She was driving home late one evening through the mountains. A highway she'd driven hundreds of times before, but it had been raining and the asphalt was slick. The car skidded on a curve and slid over the edge. If she hadn't been strapped inside, she might have had a chance. As it was...well, now you can see how I feel."

Yes, Maureen could now see a lot of things she hadn't understood before. "You must have felt like the whole world had been knocked out from under you."

"For a long time, I didn't care about anything," he admitted. "And then once I saw I had no choice but to go on living, I decided the best thing I could do was never again set myself up for that kind of loss."

Maureen's heart ached as she imagined the grief and pain he must have endured. And ached, too, because he'd gone all these years without getting over his fiancée's death.

"So you decided to close off your heart to all women."

Looking away from her, he scrubbed both hands over his face. "It was easier just to have girlfriends."

"And let everyone believe you'd simply turned into a playboy."

"I guess I did turn into one," he murmured, then turned his head and caught her gaze with his. "Until I met you."

She groaned with torment and quickly twisted away from the raw hunger on his face.

"Adam, you've carried the memory of this woman around with you all this time. It's...hard for me to believe you can let her go now. Because of me."

Before Maureen could guess his intentions, she was back in his arms, and his cheek was pressed to hers as he whispered huskily, "That's because what I feel for you is stronger than anything I suffered over Susan. It's strong enough to make me see I have to have you in my life. I don't have any choice in the matter."

Maureen desperately wanted to believe him. If she thought he truly loved her, maybe she could find the courage to try to have the family she'd always wanted. But right now, she could only see that he'd been a terribly wounded man and she wasn't at all sure she was woman enough to heal him.

She pulled away from him and scooted back behind the steering wheel. "The rain is letting up. We can't stay here all night on the side of the highway."

He stared at her with complete dismay. "That's all you have to say?"

She made herself reach for the key in the ignition. "What would you have me say?" she asked miserably.

His fingers closed tightly around her upper arm. Hardly able to breathe, she raised her eyes and looked at him in the darkness of the cab. Tension danced between them like the bolts of electricity lighting up the distant sky.

"That you love me and need me. That nothing matters but us. That you'll make love to me here and now!"

The ferocity of his voice stunned her as much as what he was saying. Her hand fell from the ignition at the same time as his name broke from her lips like a sob. He reached for her and dragged her across to his side of the seat where she went willingly into his arms.

His hands dived into her tangled hair and cradled the back of her head as he spoke against her lips. "You do want me. Tell me!"

"Yes."

That one word was all he needed to propel him into action. His lips crushed down on hers while his hands slid beneath the hem of her blouse and pressed against the warm flesh of her back.

To have him touching her, kissing her, was the only thing that eased the fire in her body, the ache in her heart. She'd wanted him for so long and had fought with herself just as long not to give in to the desire he fueled in her. But now she'd grown so weary, so raw and ragged from fighting that all she wanted was to forget and lose herself in his hard body.

In the back of her mind, she realized they were listing sideways, and moments later she felt her back against the seat. Adam lifted his head and watched her face as he undid the buttons of her blouse, then his head dipped and his tongue marked a moist path over the exposed flesh of her breasts.

Gripped by white-hot desire, she was helpless to stop their reckless plunge. She hadn't kissed him nearly enough, smelled the erotic male scent of his skin or felt his hard body enough to satisfy the hunger inside her. She wasn't sure she would ever get enough of him.

And then, just as his hand found the throbbing juncture between her thighs, his head jerked up. Maureen's eyes flew open to see the gleam of headlights sweeping through the dark interior of the cab.

Muttering several curse words, Adam pulled her blouse back together over her naked breasts.

"Has someone stopped?" she asked in a voice still husky with desire.

"No," he growled as he moved away from her. "But we have."

She fumbled with her clothing as she straightened

in the seat and her head began to swirl with the realization of just how close they'd come to making love. And this time, Adam had put an end to it!

Her heated face flaming, she jerked open the door and climbed down to the ground. Rain was still falling but at a much lighter rate. It soaked her hair and her cotton shirt as she fumbled with the last of the buttons and drew in several deep breaths of fresh air.

"Maureen, what in hell are you doing?"

She glanced over her shoulder to see that he'd joined her outside. "Trying get away from you," she answered in a desperate voice.

"Why?"

She whirled around to face him. "Because I can't trust myself with you anymore! I almost made love to you here on the side of the highway! You make me crazy! Crazy!"

Seeing it was going to take more than a few words to calm her, he took her by the shoulder. "Come on. We've got to get out of this rain and leave this place."

"Where? We're out in the middle of nowhere!"

"There's a company trailer at the rig site. It's a few miles east of here. We can stay there tonight. It's closer than driving back to town."

"No! I'm not staying anywhere with you tonight."

His fingers bit deeper into her flesh. "You won't even know I'm there."

Maureen wanted to curse at him, at herself and the whole wretched situation. But she didn't. In spite of everything that had just happened, she was here on a job as a paid geologist. She had to remember that. Gritting her teeth, she nodded. "All right. Let's go."

Fifteen minutes later, Maureen followed Adam's

truck onto the rig site. The tall derrick was brightly lit and she could see a roughneck dressed in a slicker working the catwalk in the pouring rain.

Nothing stopped a drilling rig, she thought wryly, not lightning or downpours, wind, hail, sleet or snow. Once the drill pipe bit into the earth, it was a frantic race to find gas or oil as quickly as possible. The bosses pushed their men to the limit, and the company men, such as Adam, pushed the bosses to drive them even harder. Yet she knew he asked them to do no more than what he would do himself. He was a fair man on the job. It was the deeper personal part of him that she couldn't yet trust.

They parked their vehicles beside a small trailer set up in an out-of-the-way spot away from the derrick. The sound of the rain coupled with the loud hum of the nearby generators kept the two of them from saying anything until they stepped inside.

"The bathroom is right beyond the kitchen," Adam said as he turned to her. "And the bedrooms are on either end. Take your pick. As for tomorrow, I told the old man you'd meet with him by eight. Is that okay with you?"

Maureen had been through so much in the past few hours she'd almost forgotten why she'd come here to Oklahoma in the first place. It certainly hadn't been to fall into Adam's arms. But since that had already happened, she couldn't take it back. She now had to decide what to do about him and her and the rest of her life.

"You aren't coming with me?" she asked.

He shook his head. "I left him none too happy yesterday. I don't think it would be a good idea to show my face to him again in the morning."

"I'm not so sure seeing my face is going to do the trick, either," she said wearily.

For the first time that night, he smiled at her and Maureen's heart melted a little bit more as he lifted her hand and gently kissed the back of it. "At least you're willing to try. And I thank you for that much."

She hadn't expected such tender gratitude from him, and along with the emotional ride she'd just taken with him, it was all she could do to keep from breaking down in tears.

"I'll do my best. Good night, Adam," she said quietly, then turned and headed toward the safety of the bedroom.

When Maureen woke the next morning, she was amazed that she'd slept at all. Between the rain and the deafening noise of the rig, never mind her frazzled state of mind, she'd never expected to sleep for even five minutes. Thankfully, she'd managed to catch two hours of rest.

Her watch read five-thirty Mountain Time, which meant it was already six-thirty here. She had to get up and get ready. It would never do to have an angry landowner waiting for her.

Once she'd washed and dressed, she went out to the living-dining area of the small quarters. A note was propped on the Formica table. She lifted it and began to read.

Maureen, I've gone to check on another Sanders rig about fifteen miles from here. You have the directions to the old man's house. I don't think you'll have any problem finding it. We'll talk later when you get back.

Adam

So he was already gone—she wouldn't be seeing him this morning, Maureen realized as she crumpled the note in her hand. She didn't know whether she was disappointed or relieved. After last night, she didn't know what she was thinking or feeling. All the things she'd once believed about Adam had been turned around in her mind.

The only thing she was sure about was that she loved him. And now she had to decide whether she could find the courage to stay in Ruidoso and become his wife—or go back to Houston and live the rest of her life without him.

Chapter Ten

The meeting with the landowner turned out to be far more stressful than Maureen had anticipated. He was stubborn, opinionated and, even worse, very ignorant about the environment.

However, after much talk and assurances from Maureen that his Dominicker hens wouldn't quit laying after the seismograph holes were shot and that his water well wouldn't be poisoned, he softened and agreed to let the crew do their work. The old man even invited her to stay for lunch, and Maureen ended up eating a plate of cabbage and corn bread and fried salt pork before she finally thanked him and bade him goodbye.

By the time she returned to the rig site, Adam was still gone. Maureen decided it was all for the best. Whenever he was near, she couldn't think straight. And that was the one thing she had to do now.

Quickly, she gathered up her few belongings and sat down to write him a note.

* * *

It was late afternoon before Adam finally managed to wind up his meeting with the tool pusher and drive back to the site where he'd left Maureen sleeping early that morning.

The moment he realized her pickup truck wasn't parked beside the little trailer, he got a sick feeling in the pit of his stomach. She should have been back hours ago.

As soon as he stepped inside the makeshift living quarters, he saw her note propped in the same spot he'd left his earlier. Like a hungry hound, he snatched it up and began to read.

Adam, you'll be pleased to know everything is okay with the landowner now. He was tough, but I don't think you'll be having any more problems with him.

As for me and you, I realize we can't keep going as we are. I can see I'm making you unhappy, and that's the last thing I want for you. You deserve much more than I've been able to give you.

I'll be catching the charter back to Ruidoso tonight.

Maureen

And after that? Adam wondered wildly as he gripped the small piece of paper. Why hadn't she said more?

I realize we can't keep going as we are. What in hell was she planning to do? Leave Ruidoso and Sanders? Leave him?

Grimly, he tossed the note into the trash, grabbed his duffel bag and slammed out of the little trailer.

Mercifully, the skies between Oklahoma City and Ruidoso had cleared, making the trip in the small twin-engine plane smooth and uneventful.

For a while through the flight, Maureen tried to concentrate on the extra work she'd brought with her, but after several minutes passed and she was unable to focus her thoughts on one word, she put the test reports back in her duffel bag.

With little more than two hours of sleep the night before, she felt close to being punch-drunk with exhaustion. Yet she knew trying to sleep would be just as futile as trying to work. So that left Maureen with nothing to do but stare out the window at the great plains below and try to come to terms with the agony in her heart.

She could no longer deny that she loved Adam or even that he loved her. Last night, she'd heard it in his voice, felt it in his fear, tasted it in his kiss. But was he really ready and willing to let his fiancée's ghost die?

Maureen groaned inwardly, then leaned her head back against the cushioned seat and closed her eyes. Who was she kidding? she wondered. The issue wasn't with Adam anymore. It was with herself.

For ten years, she'd carried the ghost of her baby daughter in her heart. For just as long, she'd hated herself for allowing her to die and hated David for not being the man she'd believed him to be. She'd refused to find the courage to put the tragedy behind her and make a future for herself. She couldn't blame Adam for doing the same thing.

"Ma'am, you'd better buckle up," the pilot called back to her. "We're almost at the airport."

She thanked him, and as she fastened the black safety strap across her lap, a soft smile tilted her lips. For the first time in ten years, she knew what her heart needed most and she knew with utter certainty what she had to do.

When Adam drove up the mountain to Maureen's house, it was growing close to midnight. Through the curtains, he could see one lone light burning in the living room, yet even if the house had been dark, it wouldn't have stopped him from climbing the stepping stones and banging his fist on the front door.

"Maureen, it's me, Adam! Open up!"

Several moments passed without a response, so he tried the knob and found the door unlocked. The moment he stepped inside he felt as if someone had slammed him in the gut with a broadax. Boxes and bags were piled everywhere. Mounds of clothes and books and knickknacks filled the couch and chairs.

Adam turned cold then hot as fury and fear rushed through him like a runaway freight train. She was leaving! Damn it, how could she do this to him? To herself?

"Maureen!"

Her name bellowed from his lips and this time he got a faint answer from a room in the back of the house.

"I'm in here, Adam."

He followed the muted sound down the hallway to the room he knew she'd chosen for her bedroom. When he entered the open door, he saw much the same mess he'd found in the living room. Clothes, shoes, books and linens were piled and draped everywhere.

Spotting the movement of her arm in the walk-in closet, he started across the room. As he did, he noticed the picture of baby Elizabeth and the small quilt was lying on the corner of the bed along with a few other odds and ends. The sight of the objects made him wince inside. He knew she'd been hurt as no woman should ever have to hurt. But that was behind her now. He had to make her see reason.

"Maureen, what the hell are you doing?"

She looked up to see him standing in the doorway of the closet. He wasn't wearing a hat and his dark auburn hair shone like bronze beneath the glare of the lightbulb. A lock of it fell onto his furrowed brow, and as her gaze traveled downward, she noticed his face was as rigid as a piece of granite. Exhaustion and anger shadowed his eyes and his lips were nothing but a flat, grim line. But he'd never looked better to Maureen, and it was all she could do to keep from smiling at him. Even more, to keep from flinging herself into his arms.

"I'm packing," she said as casually as she could manage.

"Packing? Packing? It was only a few weeks ago I helped you unpack! Are you never going to quit running away, Maureen?"

She stepped out of the closet and tossed an armful of clothes onto the already loaded bed. "Who said anything about running?"

"Nobody had to! I'm not blind, Maureen. You left Oklahoma like a scalded cat just so you wouldn't have to face me!"

With her hands on her hips, she tilted her chin up

and looked him in the eye. "I had some thinking to do."

A sneer twisted his features. "And I guess you decided running from me like a coward was the easiest way out. Where are you going? Back to Houston?"

"I never want to go back to Houston."

Confusion suddenly flickered in his eyes. "Then where are you going?"

Adam's eyes drifted up and down the length of her as she gave him a negligible shrug. She was wearing a simple dress of pale blue cotton. Buttons started at the low neckline just above her breasts and ended at the hemline at her ankles. The sight of her luscious curves fueled the need boiling inside him.

"I'm not sure if the place has a name. If I heard it, I don't recall it. Anyway," she went on as she turned and picked up a sweater from the end of the bed and tossed it into a nearby box, "it's somewhere in the mountains and the owner had the goofy idea that a couple of carpenters could turn the house into a home."

Suddenly, his hands were on her shoulders and spinning her around to face him. "Maureen, are you...playing with me?"

She couldn't hold herself back any longer. She chuckled softly and stepped into his arms. "Only for the rest of my life."

Adam's arms crushed her to him and for long moments he held her fast against his pounding heart. "How did you—I thought—oh, God, Maureen, I thought you were leaving me."

She shook her head resolutely. "Last night, I didn't want to admit what has been staring me in the face for a long time. I love you, Adam. I don't want to live my life without you.''

The air whooshed out of him on a groan of triumph, then, his expression grave, he tilted her face up to his. "You've been adamant about not wanting to marry or have children. Have you really changed your mind?''

She swallowed as an overwhelming surge of love filled her throat with tears of joy. "Oh, Adam, I guess I'd been living in the past for so long that when I met you I didn't know how to look toward the future. And then when you tried to make me see how things really were, I was afraid to try to look or plan or hope.''

With a groan of disbelief, his head fell back. "So why didn't you stay at the rig and wait for me? Your note implied—I didn't know what the hell to think. The past five hours traveling home has been pure torture!''

"I'm so sorry, Adam. But I was going through some torture of my own. Last night when you told me about Susan, I couldn't help but think you weren't over her, that you couldn't possibly love me. And then I realized I couldn't hold it against you for carrying her ghost around all this time. I've been doing the same thing with Elizabeth's memory.''

His head lowered and his eyes searched hers. "Oh, Maureen, I haven't loved Susan for a long time. In fact, now that I've fallen in love with you, I'm not sure what I felt for her was true, adult love. We were both very young, and I think I was consumed with the idea of being grown up with a wife and children of my own. When Susan's death took that dream away, I didn't have the courage to try to find it again. Not until you came along.''

Her arms tightened around him and she pressed her cheek against the beat of his heart. "This afternoon I realized losing you through my own stubbornness would be much worse than losing you through an accident or illness." At his sudden chuckle, she tilted her head back to look at him. "Is that so funny?"

His thumb and forefinger gave her chin a little tweak. "You've already tried to kill me down in South America and you couldn't manage to do it. That ought to prove I'd be a hard man to get rid of."

Laughing, she lifted her hand and touched his face. He was the most gorgeous, exciting man she'd ever met, but that was only a part of why she loved him. He understood her. He needed and wanted her and he would always be there for her. Just knowing that melted her heart with a joy so pure and sweet she wanted to weep.

"So when can we move to your house?" she asked. "As you can see, I've already started packing. Are the carpenters finished yet?"

His grin was full of sensual promise. "If they aren't already, we'll run them off and finish it ourselves."

"And what about getting married? Do you want a big ceremony with your family or..." She stopped abruptly as he began to laugh. With a puzzled frown, she asked, "You do want to get married, don't you? Or are you playing with me now?"

The look he shot her said he couldn't wait to get his hands on her. "Of course I want to get married, darling! You're going to be my wife, and we're going to have as many children as God will allow," he said soberly, then with a joyous chuckle, he added, "I was laughing because I suddenly realized why we happened to meet up again here in Ruidoso."

Puzzled, she shook her head. "There's nothing odd about my coming here. I work in the gas and oil business. Sanders needed a geologist and your father—"

"No! No! It wasn't any of that. It was that damn bridal bouquet!"

Maureen stared at him as if he'd just lost his mind. "A bridal bouquet! What are you talking about?"

"My sister Anna. I came home from South America to attend her wedding. At that time, my ankle was still in a cast, and when she tossed her bouquet, I couldn't get out of the way fast enough. I ended up catching it! Hell, I should've known something like this was going to happen to me!"

Maureen burst into laughter. "Oh, Adam, you catching the bouquet, that's hilarious! Do you still have it? I'd love to see this piece of fate that brought us together."

He shook his head and grinned. "No. I tossed it to my cousin Caroline." His eyes suddenly widened as he looked down at Maureen. "Dear Lord, I wonder what's going to happen to her?"

With a contented sigh, Maureen went up on her tiptoes and raised her lips to his. "I can only hope it's as wonderful as this."

* * * * *

SOMETIMES THE SMALLEST PACKAGES CAN LEAD TO THE BIGGEST SURPRISES!

Bundles of Joy

February 1999
A VOW, A RING, A BABY SWING
by Teresa Southwick (SR #1349)

Pregnant and alone, Rosie Marchetti had just been stood up at the altar. So family friend Steve Schafer stepped up the aisle and married her. Now Rosie is trying to convince him that this family was meant to be....

May 1999
THE BABY ARRANGEMENT
by Moyra Tarling (SR #1368)

Jared McAndrew has been searching for his son, and when he discovers Faith Nelson with his child he demands she come home with him. Can Faith convince Jared that he has the wrong mother—but the right bride?

Enjoy these stories of love and family. And look for future BUNDLES OF JOY titles from Leanna Wilson and Suzanne McMinn coming in the fall of 1999.

BUNDLES OF JOY
only from

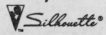
Silhouette®

Available wherever Silhouette books are sold.

If you enjoyed what you just read,
then we've got an offer you can't resist!

Take 2 bestselling
love stories FREE!
Plus get a FREE surprise gift!

CATCH
THE
BOUQUET!

These delightful stories of love and
passion, by three of the romance world's bestselling
authors, will make you look back on your own wedding
with a smile—or give you some ideas for a future one!

THE MAN SHE
MARRIED

by

ANN MAJOR

EMMA DARCY

ANNETTE
BROADRICK

Available at your favorite retail outlet.

Silhouette
ROMANCE™

COMING NEXT MONTH

#1372 I MARRIED THE BOSS!—Laura Anthony
Loving the Boss
Sophia Shepherd wanted to marry the ideal man, and her new boss, Rex Michael Barrington III, was as dreamy as they came! But when an overheard conversation had him testing her feelings, Sophia had to prove she wanted more than just a dream....

#1373 HIS TEN-YEAR-OLD SECRET—Donna Clayton
Fabulous Fathers
Ten years of longing were over. Tess Galloway had returned to claim the child she'd thought lost to her forever. But Dylan Minster, her daughter's father and the only man she'd ever loved, would not let Tess have her way without a fight, and without her heart!

#1374 THE RANCHER AND THE HEIRESS—Susan Meier
Texas Family Ties
City girl Alexis MacFarland wasn't thrilled about spending a year on a ranch—even if it meant she'd inherit half of it! But one look at ranch owner Caleb Wright proved it wouldn't be *that* bad, *if* she could convince him she'd be his cowgirl for good.

#1375 THE MARRIAGE STAMPEDE—Julianna Morris
Wranglers & Lace
Wrangler Merrie Foster and stockbroker Logan Kincaid were *nothing* alike. She wanted kids and country life, and he wanted wealth and the city. But when they ended up in a mock engagement, would the sparks between them overcome their differences?

#1376 A BRIDE IN WAITING—Sally Carleen
On the Way to a Wedding
Stand in for a missing bride? Sara Martin didn't mind, especially as a favor for Dr. Lucas Daniels. But when her life became filled with wedding plans and stolen kisses, Sara knew she wanted to change from stand-in bride to wife forever!

#1377 HUSBAND FOUND—Martha Shields
Family Matters
Single mother Emma Lockwood needed a job...and R. D. Johnson was offering one. Trouble was, Rafe was Emma's long-lost husband—and he didn't recognize her! Could she help him recover his memory—and the love they once shared?